Ayla Asher xoxo

Hearts Reclaimed

Ardor Creek, Book 1

By

AYLA ASHER

Contents

Cover Design: Anthony O'Brien, www.BookCoverDesign.store

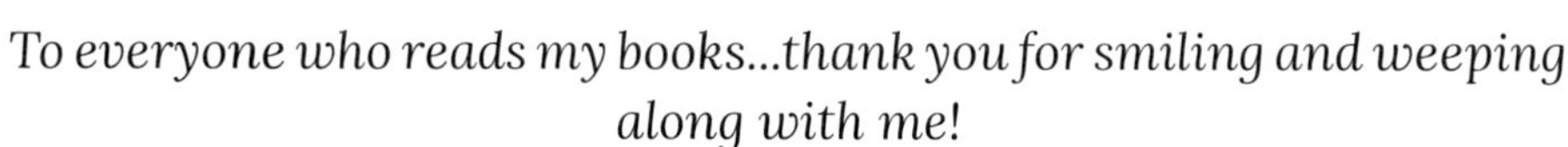

To everyone who reads my books...thank you for smiling and weeping along with me!

A Note from the Author

Hello, lovely readers! I'm so excited to bring you this new series. For those of you who've read and supported the Manhattan Holiday Loves series, thank you from the bottom of my heart. That friend family is awesome and I love hearing how they made you smile and maybe shed a tear or two at points!

For this new series, I decided to do something a bit different. I've wanted to write a love story about a widower ever since I fell in love with Jude Law's character in The Holiday. Of course, it's a difficult subject with lots of complexities that must be handled with care. I did my best to tackle the heavy themes with thoughtfulness and diligence, and really enjoyed writing Scott and Ashlyn's story. Here's hoping you fall in love with them like I did.

I set out to make this new series fun and lighthearted but it turned out to be a bit more emotional than I thought. Since 2020 has been an emotional whirlwind for us all, I figured I'd embrace it. I'm pretty sure Carrie and Peter's book is going to be a tear-jerker too and I can't wait to bring it to you. For now, happy reading as you get to know Scott and Ashlyn!

Chapter 1

Ashlyn Rivers drove her sporty compact sedan through the small town square. The sidewalks were lined with businesses one would expect from any American hamlet: drugstore, diner, hair salon, and so on. Mentally checking them off in her mind, she noted the immaculate signage and clean streets. Grandma Jean had loved this town and had a fondness for the mayor, who'd passed several local ordinances to ensure the business owners hung signs with the same fonts and colors. Ardor Creek, Pennsylvania had been Jean's home for eighty-two years and now it was Ashlyn's.

Heart filled with trepidation at starting over, Ashlyn took several deep breaths as she passed the tall clock situated at the northernmost point of the main square. Veering onto the two-lane road, she continued down the street, not another car in sight, although it was three in the afternoon and the sun sat high in the blue sky.

Searching the horizon, she saw the small gravel road that led to her grandma's house. Turning onto it, her body vibrated along with the car over the rocky path. After passing the woods that surrounded the home, she pulled up in front of the house, craning her neck to look at the dilapidated structure.

"Well, Ashlyn, you wanted an adventure," she muttered. "Might as well get on with it." Stepping from the car, she pushed the door shut and tentatively approached the house. Sticking her hands in the back pockets of her jeans, she marveled at the project she'd undertaken.

Some might say she was running, and that was just fine. They didn't understand her circumstances and they'd never met Grandma Jean. The woman was a firecracker and Ashlyn had loved her more than anyone. When she'd passed away a month ago, Ashlyn had expected her to leave the house to her parents or her uncle. Instead, she'd left it to her only granddaughter, shocking the family. As her eyes wandered over the home, Ashlyn felt a tug deep in her bones. A reminder of the times she and Jean had shared. Grandma was convinced a spirit haunted the century-old home and Ashlyn had shared her beliefs. Now, she was going to renovate so the house could be added to Ardor Creek's haunted homes tour. It was a popular fall attraction in the rural town and would give her some much-needed publicity for her mobile restaurant.

Somewhere along the way she'd gotten the idea that she wanted to buy a food truck and create an organic mobile restaurant...in a brand new town...two and a half hours from Manhattan in the middle of Pennsylvania. Good lord, she was certifiably insane.

Rubbing her forehead, she continued to study the house, understanding it needed a ton of work. Jean spent her last two years in assisted living and the house had been vacant that entire time. It would need a complete overhaul and renovation. Thank goodness she had a crap ton of money saved from the corporate job she'd resigned from two weeks ago. It wouldn't last forever but it was a healthy chunk and would help her get on her feet with the new business and the house.

Crossing her fingers inside her jean pocket, she willed that sentiment to be true. It was okay to make mistakes—that was inevitable—but she couldn't fall on her ass completely. Success was her only option. Lifting her chin with determination, she embraced her future.

"All right, Ashlyn, enough staring. Time to make good on all those promises you made yourself." Steeled with determination from the self-pep-talk, she grabbed her bag from the car and trailed up the rickety front porch steps, spine straight and head held high.

Chapter 2

Ashlyn was pleased to find the water still worked, although it ran brown for a good five minutes from each faucet before finally turning clear. She'd helped Jean with the bills and driven from Manhattan to check on the house every few months, so she knew it was habitable. Still, it was old and full of creaks and groans, which she found incredibly exciting. Ashlyn loved a good ghost story and was enthralled by the spirit that supposedly lived in Grandma Jean's home. *Her* home now.

First, she needed to secure a contractor. After hours spent combing the internet, she'd decided upon Scott Grillo of Grillo Design and Construction. The firm had rave reviews and seemed to be the most prominent in Ardor Creek. If she was going to blow her money on renovations, might as well blow it on the best firm. After a sound sleep on the freshly washed sheets she'd thrown upon her grandma's bed, Ashlyn rose with the sun and headed into town to get a quote. Her former job as a pharmaceutical sales rep had instilled her with a love of negotiation—and successful negotiation was always best achieved face to face.

After parking her car in one of the empty spots that ran along Main Street's sidewalk, she located the business and headed inside.

"Can I help you?" The receptionist gave her a warm smile under a mop of curly red hair that fell to her shoulders.

"Yes, I'd like to meet with Scott Grillo please."

The woman's green eyes widened. "Do you have an appointment?'

"No," Ashlyn said, maintaining her polite but assertive tone, "but I'm new in town and figured I'd take a shot at tracking him down in the office. I was hoping he wouldn't be out on a job yet since it's still pretty early."

The receptionist blinked a few times, processing. "Where are you from?" Her jaw moved as she worked the gum in between her teeth.

"New York City, although my Grandma Jean lived here for over eighty years."

"Jean Rivers?"

"Yep. Did you know her?"

"Oh, man, she was sweet and salty at the same time. I loved seeing her at all the parades and town gatherings. I heard she passed about a month ago. I'm so sorry, sweetie."

Ashlyn gave a sad smile. "Thank you."

Standing, she extended her hand. "I'm Carrie Longwood, Scott's assistant. I just adored Jean. We all did."

"She was one of my favorite people in the world, that's for sure," she said, shaking her hand. "I've moved into her home and am looking to renovate it. Seems like Mr. Grillo is the best and I don't want to settle for anything less."

"He sure is." Lowering into the chair, she maneuvered the mouse and perused the computer screen. "He's not here yet but should be in any minute. He won't be doing site visits until later today. But I have to warn you..."

"Yes?" Ashlyn asked when she trailed off.

"Well, Scott's a little surly." Glancing to the ceiling, she contemplated before returning her gaze to Ashlyn's. "Actually, he's a lot surly. Doesn't really deal with new customers face to face. He usually has me or Peter do that."

"Peter Stratford? I saw his name on your website."

"That's him," Carrie said with a nod. "He grew up here but moved to the city to become a fancy Wall Street broker. Eventually, he burnt out and moved back home. Scott snatched him up to utilize those fancy financial skills and good looks at GDC."

Ashlyn glanced at the business cards atop the counter, realizing that GDC stood for Grillo Design and Construction. "I understand but I also have a background in sales and always found it's best to negotiate with the decision-maker. So, if it's all the same to you, I'd like to wait until Mr. Grillo comes in and speak to him directly."

White teeth flashed as Carrie smacked her gum. "Oh, yeah. He won't know what to do with you. You just sit right down over there and we'll catch him when he walks in, Ms. Rivers. It is Rivers, right?"

"Yes, Grandma Jean was my Dad's mom, but you can call me Ashlyn."

"Well, pleasure to meet you, Ashlyn. I like your New York City swagger. We don't get many city people out here."

"I'm pretty blunt but also want to make a good impression. Tell me if I'm blowing it, okay, Carrie?"

"Ten-four," she said with a salute.

Shooting her a grin, Ashlyn sat down in one of the plastic chairs, pulling out her phone to scroll through Instagram while she waited. Tamping down the urge to search Robert's profile, she absently kicked her crossed leg as she caught up on the posts. The bell above the door rang and a man entered carrying a briefcase but otherwise dressed semi-casually in jeans and a button-down shirt. His lips twitched—not quite a grin—at Carrie before his gaze fell to her. Brown irises roved over Ashlyn beneath his brown-rimmed glasses. Glancing back at Carrie, he muttered, "Why is there a strange woman sitting in our office?"

Standing, Ashlyn approached, extending a hand. "Ashlyn Rivers, Mr. Grillo. A pleasure to meet you. I'm here to hire you to renovate my grandma's home."

Chestnut eyebrows drew together as he studied her, staring at her outstretched hand as if she were offering him a palmful of poisonous snakes instead of a handshake. "We're not taking on new clients until August. Carrie, set up an appointment for her to meet with Peter." Dismissing her, he turned and began to charge toward the back.

"Um, excuse me," she said, grabbing his arm. "But I'm only interested in meeting with you."

He froze, slowly rotating to glare at her fingers encircling his forearm. Lifting his hand, he extricated her grasp, finger by finger, until she released him.

"Sorry, but this project is going to be expensive and I won't settle for anything less than the best. I'm pretty stubborn so it's probably best if you just sit down and meet with me for a few minutes."

Silence blanketed the room, the only movements a tick of a muscle in his firm jaw and the rhythm of the second hand on the large clock that hung on the wall. Finally, he spoke, the words low and annoyed. "Listen, lady, I don't care who you are, how stubborn you are, or what the hell you think you're entitled to. I run my business in a systematic manner and Peter Stratford conducts our new client meetings. You can meet with him or you can consult some other contractors. Have a good day." With a nod, he pivoted and stormed to the back, disappearing into what she assumed was his office.

Sucking in a breath, Ashlyn expelled it through puffed cheeks. "Well, *that* didn't go as planned."

Carrie's eyes sparkled with excited mischief. "Oh, yeah. This is good stuff. Okay, come here." She crooked a finger and Ashlyn leaned on the counter. Carrie dragged the arrow around the screen, irises darting over the schedule. "He'll be at the new construction site from three to six this afternoon. It's over on the annex that runs off Cyprus street. Most of the guys leave at three so you should have a pretty good chance of cornering him. He likes to go in once the work is done for the day and check on things. Look up 'perfectionist' in a dictionary and you'll find a picture of Scott."

"You're a saint," Ashlyn said, thrilled the woman was helping her. "I can't thank you enough."

"No prob," Carrie said, leaning back in her chair. "Scott's been stuck for a while and I have this strange feeling you might just be the one to slick him up again."

"Oh, no," Ashlyn said, hands lifted, palms facing Carrie. "I have no interest in anything but the house. I just got out of a disastrous relationship and I've sworn off men for good."

"So have I, but that doesn't mean I don't want them to at least *try* to get into my knickers."

Laughing, Ashlyn shook her head. "Not me. I'm done...for a while at least. But I appreciate the info. How mad will he be when I show up there?"

Squinting at the ceiling, Carrie said, "Somewhere between a hornet and a rattlesnake."

Ashlyn grinned, wondering why the idea of ruffling the stoic man's feathers gave her such an excited thrill. "Awesome. Wish me luck."

"Good luck, honey. Give him hell. Stop by again sometime and tell me how it went."

"Will do." Grabbing a business card, Ashlyn all but skipped out the door, stretching her arms wide under the morning sun. Birds chirped back under the late-March sky and a car lazily trailed down the quiet main street. "Phase One, underway. Nice job, Rivers. Keep it up." Ready to face the day, she grabbed a sandwich at the deli before heading home to resume cleaning her new house.

Chapter 3

Ashlyn resembled a tornado in the hours that followed, wanting to ensure the house was spotless. Of course, parts would be torn up during renovation but she still liked living in a tidy home. As she assessed the two-story dwelling, she took stock of what needed to be done. Both bathrooms needed to be completely gutted but the two upstairs bedrooms were fine. The fireplace in the living room needed work but, otherwise, she could leave that room alone for now. She wanted to completely redo the den and make it into an office and the kitchen needed to be revamped with a bigger oven, new cabinets and counters, and updated appliances. The upstairs attic would remain untouched but the front porch needed to be completely redone. Satisfied with her assessment, she looked at the list she'd written in the notebook wondering how much it was going to cost.

"You'll just have to negotiate, Ashlyn," she murmured, trailing her finger over the black scribbles, trying not to hyperventilate at the amount of money she was going to spend. There was always reward at the end of risk—she firmly believed this—and was determined to see the renovation through.

Peeking at her phone, she realized it was almost four o'clock. Well past time for her to track down Mr. Grumpy Contractor and try again to solidify his commitment to work with her. Trailing to the bathroom, she applied some eyeliner for good measure. One thing she'd learned during her tenure in sales was that it never hurt to sharpen one's appearance. Giving her reflection a satisfied nod, she grabbed her purse and headed toward her car.

After locating the construction site on the map application of her phone, she plopped it in the holder attached to the dashboard and began her journey. Ten minutes later, she pulled to a stop on the dirt road in front of the half-built home. Stepping from the car, she slid her phone in her back jeans pocket, thinking it would be good to have handy just in case. After all, she was walking into an active construction site. If something fell on her head, she should probably have a way to call 911.

Glancing around, she noticed the site was all but deserted. A porta-john sat off to the right, as well as three foundations that had been poured for other homes. Taking in the site, she realized it would eventually be a pretty new neighborhood, perfect for young families or people wishing to retire from the bustle of the city. Tentatively trailing up the wooden stairs of the almost-finished front porch, Ashlyn entered through the open doorway.

"Hello? Mr. Grillo? It's Ashlyn Rivers. Are you here?"

Perking her ears, she heard a small clanking sound and followed it. As she navigated down the hallway, she came upon a bathroom that looked to be nearly completed. Unable to squelch the small gasp, she lifted her fingers to her lips.

Scott Grillo stood on a ladder, shirtless, arms stretched high as he maneuvered a screwdriver into one of the ceiling light fixtures. Focused with laser concentration on the task, he didn't seem to notice her presence. Not wanting to startle him, she waited, allowing her to take in the stunning magnificence of Mr. Sexy Contractor's chest.

Broad shoulders sat below magnificent arms with straining biceps as he fidgeted. Small rivulets of sweat dripped from his pecs, covered by springy brown hair, past his copper nipples and six-pack to the 'V' that led into his jeans. Swallowing thickly, Ashlyn was overcome with lust for perhaps the first time in her thirty-three years on the planet. Yes, she'd always thought Robert attractive and had enjoyed the sex, although it certainly hadn't been mind-blowing, but Scott Grillo took sex appeal to a whole new level. *Down girl*, she chided herself, flexing her fingers so the tight fists she'd formed wouldn't cut off her circulation. Realizing she was staring like a creepy stalker, she lightly cleared her throat.

His head snapped toward her and the ladder began to wobble. Jumping into action, she rushed forward, grabbing the metal legs to still the contraption. Lifting her gaze, she observed a livid Scott Grillo glowering down at her.

"Hi," she said cheerfully, giving him a wave. "Figured I'd track you down for that meeting."

Firm nostrils flared as his jaw clenched. "You're trespassing."

She squinted one eye, trying to keep her tone light. "Yeah, probably. But I figure you'll have to climb down to call the cops. Once I have you on solid ground, I can at least meet with you until they arrest me."

Giving her a droll look, he sighed and climbed down the ladder. As he faced her, Ashlyn told herself *not* to look at his chest. His magnificently glistening chest...

"Look, lady—"

"Ashlyn," she said, lifting her chin. "I'd prefer it if you call me Ashlyn. 'Lady' is a bit rude."

Setting the screwdriver on the counter, he crossed his arms over that glorious chest and arched an eyebrow. "*You're* lecturing *me* on rude? Do you understand that you're breaking about seventeen laws by showing up here?"

Her features scrunched. "I think seventeen is a bit excessive. Although, I'm certainly trespassing. Sorry about that, by the way. If you give me five minutes, I promise I'll leave you alone...until you show up to work on my house, that is."

Those deep brown eyes darted between hers. "You really think you can convince me to take on a new job that I have absolutely no time for in five minutes flat?"

"Sure do," she said with a nod. "Where should we negotiate. Front porch?"

With a slight eye roll, he tilted his head. "Fine."

Responding with a glowing smile, she pivoted, hoping he'd follow her outside. Sure enough, he exited a moment later, sliding his shirt over his arms and buttoning several of the lower buttons. *Bummer.* Ashlyn would've really enjoyed seeing that chest in the waning afternoon sunlight but figured fortune had other ideas. Still, she likely wouldn't forget it anytime soon. Maybe she'd dream about it tonight and dig up some batteries for the vibrator she'd packed. After all, a woman had needs and that wouldn't violate the celibacy pact she'd forced on herself after the disaster with Robert…

"Well, I think you've got four minutes left," Scott said, crossing his arms as he leaned against the porch railing.

"Mr. Grillo—"

"Scott is fine."

"Thank you," she said with a nod. "Scott, as you might have figured out, I'm like a dog with a bone when I decide on something. I've decided I'd like to hire you to renovate my grandma's home. You might have known her. Jean Rivers?"

His features softened. "Yes, I remember her. She always brought me cookies when she came into town, especially after…" Trailing off, he scowled. "Well, anyway, she was nice. I think she moved into the assisted living home in Scranton a few years ago, right? How's she doing?"

"She passed away about a month ago."

Compassion entered his eyes. "I'm sorry. She was a lovely woman."

"Thank you," Ashlyn said, feeling her throat bob. "She really was." Exhaling a breath, she looked out over the site before lifting her gaze to his. "I've moved into her home and will be renovating it in the hopes of having it added to the local haunted homes tour. Grandma Jean was convinced a ghost resided there."

His lips curved into a soft grin. "I've heard the story. The woman who lived there lost her husband in World War I. It was said she wept for his return until she died of a broken heart. Her body was found in the attic in an old rocker, still swaying as she clutched her chest."

Ashlyn couldn't contain her smile. "Yep, that's it. Her name was Sally Pickens and I'm going to my best to honor her story and her spirit. The house needs quite a bit of work to be eligible for the tour and I'm intent on hiring you, Scott. Your ability to design and perform construction is exactly what I need since I don't plan on hiring an architect. I like my projects streamlined and want to hire one vendor who can meet my needs."

His brows lifted, perhaps at the slight double entendre, and his eyes raked over her. Feeling exposed, Ashlyn refused to back down, realizing the man must be used to intimidating those he came into contact with. Gauging him to be at least six-foot-two, he dwarfed over her five-foot, five-inch frame.

"I appreciate your interest in hiring me but I'm fully booked at the moment."

Arching a brow, she went for the kill. "Even with the loss of Charmeldee Acres to the corporate construction firm in Scranton?"

His eyes narrowed. "How do you know about that?"

"I'm a pretty good researcher and understand the firm stole the contract right out from under you. It was covered extensively by the local Scranton media outlets. Must've been a financial blow since you declined several other projects to take on that development."

"Jobs come and go. I didn't really want to take on a project that close to Scranton anyway. My business manager, Peter, urged me to bid on it and, even though we won the initial bid, I wasn't torn up when we lost it. Gives me more time to take on local projects and those are what I really enjoy."

"Great. I've got a local project all teed up and ready to go. Also, I pay in cash and have a ton of it saved up ready to place right there in your palm. So, what do you say? Want to come by the house tomorrow for a survey?"

He just stood silent, contemplating her.

"Is that a 'yes'?"

More silence.

"Hello?" she called, waving her hand in front of his face. "Cat got your tongue?"

"No. I'm just trying to recall if I've ever had a more annoying conversation in my entire life."

Ouch. Bristling, she straightened her shoulders. "I guess annoyance is better than indifference. If I have to get under your skin, I will. Like I said, when I set my mind to something, I like to see it through. And a funny thing I'm learning about small towns is that everyone's quite chatty. Like Donna at the deli, who served me a sandwich this morning. She was all too eager to tell me about her husband, Dan, who works for you as a contractor but is now on unemployment because he was slated to work on the Charmeldee Acres job." Making a *tsk, tsk, tsk* sound with her tongue, she shot him a sardonic smile. "Wouldn't it be nice if a new job appeared like that?" Snapping her fingers, she nodded. "I bet it would be."

"The answer is 'no', Ms. Rivers."

"Ashlyn, please. And if there's one thing I learned from my fancy corporate sales job, it's that each 'no' just brings you one step closer to a 'yes'." Placing her hands on her hips, she squinted. "What else did Donna tell me? Oh, yes, that half of your customers are on a payment plan and it messes like hell with your cash flow. She said you have a heart of gold under that surly exterior and let the old retired couples in town pay you monthly, sometimes for jobs that were completed years ago. I'm willing to pay in cash. Up front. Are you picking up what I'm putting down here?"

His full lips twitched, although she couldn't tell if it was from amusement or frustration. "Did you say you relocated to your grandma's home?"

"Yes. Why?"

"Because I give you a month before you run back to New York, city girl. There's no way you'll make it here. Not with a mouth and an attitude like that. Now, if you'll excuse me, I have an inspection to finish. Get off my site or I'll call the cops. They really enjoy locking up mouthy New Yorkers. You can show yourself to the car." Gesturing to her car with his head, he rotated and stormed back into the house.

Ashlyn gaped, open-mouthed, at his broad back before it disappeared inside. Sputtering at what an ass he was, she stomped down the stairs and slammed the car door shut once she was behind the wheel. "Self-important son of a bitch," she muttered, starting the car. Pumping the gas pedal, she sped off, not caring that she spewed gravel all over the site.

As she drove home, she contemplated where the conversation had gone so wrong, realizing she'd probably been a bit too aggressive. "You can take the girl out of the city but..." she murmured as she puttered along. Still, she was nothing if not persistent and figured there was still a way to get the infuriating contractor to take on the job.

At this point, she could approach one of the other contractors she'd researched but none have them had the rave reviews Scott's firm did. And, honestly, where was the fun in that? Giving up now would equal capitulation and Ashlyn Rivers never capitulated. No, she was a born salesperson and knew there was always a path to the 'yes' if one remained in dogged pursuit. Resolved to win the grumpy contractor over, she spent the rest of the night with a bottle of wine, perusing the internet to find out everything she could about Scott Grillo so she could formulate the next step in her pursuit of his exquisite ~~chest~~...er, uh, contractor skills. Right—his contractor skills. That was definitely *all* she was interested in...

Chapter 4

Ashlyn awoke and stretched in her grandma's queen-sized four-poster bed. Squishing the skin around her eyes, she realized they were still a bit swollen...which made sense she'd devolved into a sobbing pile of mush last night as she'd sat before her laptop. As the night wore on, there had been so many tears mixed with her third glass of wine, it should've been watered down. Closing her eyes at the pounding of her head, she muttered, "No such luck, Ashlyn."

After popping two ibuprofen, she sat down at the kitchen table and flipped open the computer. Pulling up the last article which she'd bookmarked, she read it again.

Christina Grillo, 32, and her daughter Ella, 2, were killed by a drunk driver on their way home from visiting Mrs. Grillo's mother in Scranton. The drunk driver, David Smith, was also pronounced dead at the scene of the accident. A funeral will be held by the Grillo family on Saturday, June 9, and details can be found below.

Gnawing her lip, Ashlyn regarded the date of the article, written over five years ago. Sadness swamped her as she remembered Scott's words from yesterday.

Your grandma always brought me cookies when she came into town, especially after...

Especially after his family's accident.

Running her hand through her hair, Ashlyn felt the tears forming again. God, life was so unfair. No wonder the president of GDC was a gruff, churlish man. How in the hell did one go on after such a horrific loss?

"Probably like a grumpy jerk," she muttered, still a bit annoyed at yesterday's conversation but also armed with compassion she hadn't possessed then. Looking at the notes she'd taken on the pad that rested beside the computer, she understood this was probably why Scott didn't have social media. She'd tried like hell to find a Facebook, Instagram, or even a Pinterest profile, but there had been none. Who wanted to be on social media where people posted pictures of their babies and smiling families twenty-four seven? Certainly not the man who'd lost his own family. It made complete sense.

Being that she wasn't wasted like she'd been last night, she quickly willed the tears to dry and stood, wondering what she should do with this newfound information. She still wanted Scott's company to perform the renovation but also didn't want to antagonize the man, whom she now had a soft spot for.

"Three days in the country and you've become a damn sap, Rivers. Nice job."

Pushing away the negative self-talk, she stood and decided she'd take a jog before determining her next move. A good run always cleared her head and helped with hangovers—both of which she sorely needed. Throwing on her sports bra, shorts, and sneakers, she stretched in the front yard before popping in the air buds to listen to the podcast she'd pulled up. Heading into the sunny spring day, she embraced the pounding of her heart and rush of air through her lungs as she jogged.

Scott lifted his head and scowled at the flash of a woman who ran past the front window of GDC. Gritting his teeth, he recalled yesterday's irritating interruption and conversation.

"Did I lose you, boss?" Carrie said below him.

"No," he said, lowering his gaze back to the screen, which he was observing over her shoulder. He'd forgotten about the follow-up appointment with Dr. Paterson tomorrow and needed to shift a few things around. "Let's reschedule Mrs. Stratton's appointment for next Wednesday," he said, pointing at the screen.

"Got it," she said, typing away with her long, red fingernails. "Rescheduled the sweet old lady who likes to pay you in pies for next Wednesday. It's really nice of you to check on her light fixture. She swears it wasn't installed properly during last year's renovation but I think she's just lonely since her husband passed away."

"I don't mind checking on her. Now that my shin splints are all but healed—which should be confirmed at tomorrow's appointment—I won't have to go in for those fittings anymore. The orthotics Doc Paterson made for me are pretty killer."

"Looks like you've got another runner in town," Carrie said, gaze darting to the window before she beamed up at him. "Maybe you two could run together."

"Not likely." Leaning on the desk, he crossed his arms over his chest. "Want to tell me how Miss Big City knew I was at the site yesterday?"

Her eyes grew wide, filled with mock innocence. "She did? Oh, my. I have absolutely no idea."

"Right. And did you also tell her about the Charmeldee Acres debacle?"

Carrie's auburn eyebrows arched. "Nope, not a word on that one, I swear. Big City Lady must've figured that one out on her own."

With an annoyed grunt, Scott pushed away from the desk. "No more schedule leaks. I appreciate the sentiment but have no desire to work with a mouthy city dweller who's only going to last weeks here."

"I wasn't necessarily pushing her toward you with the project in mind."

Scott shot her a look. "No matchmaking, Carrie. We talked about this. I'm just not interested."

Turning in her chair, she studied him. "Scott, you forget I've known you since we were kids. The way you helped me after my divorce...well, the boys love you." Glancing at the picture of her two sons on the desk, she smiled. "You deserve love and I hate that you've decided you don't. It's not what Tina would've wanted for you."

Scott felt the anger and pain well in his gut, as it always did when he allowed himself to think of his wife and daughter. Tamping it down, he shook his head. "You've got a good heart, Carrie. Channel that energy toward someone who'll appreciate it. Don't meddle in my business. I mean it."

She surprised him by emitting a chuckle. "Wow, I've really ruffled your feathers. Or, should I say, *she* really ruffled your feathers. This is gonna be good." She gave him a wink, completely unfazed by his harsh tone.

Rolling his eyes, he turned and stalked toward his office, realizing Carrie knew him too well and could read his moods with ease. "Send Peter back when he gets here. We need to talk about a few projects."

"Aye, aye, captain," came her cheerful reply.

Reminding himself not to slam the door to his office, since it was made of glass, he closed it gently while wishing he could pound his fist through it. He'd been a truculent son of a bitch lately and didn't see that getting any better with the appearance of Miss Sassy City Girl on the horizon. Pulling up his design files, he attempted to do some work before Peter appeared.

No less than five minutes later, he was googling the infuriating woman's name, trying to dig up dirt. He had no idea why—she was a nuisance who'd almost sentenced him to death-by-ladder yesterday—but he was interested for some reason. He found her on Facebook but since he didn't have an account, he couldn't see her pictures or posts. Perusing the search results, he found a few articles from her stint in Corporate America. She was pictured with her wide smile and glowing dark green eyes on stage in a plethora of pictures from sales meetings where she held various trophies. Scott noted she'd won Sales Rep of the year multiple times.

Sitting back in his leather chair, he pondered. It took a certain person to approach customers daily and deal with a multitude of rejections until you made a sale. A reluctant admiration washed over him as he realized he never would've been able to do that job.

No, that's why he'd hired Peter to be the head of sales and finance when he'd returned home from his uppity Wall Street job. Scott just didn't enjoy negotiation and sales. Carrie had been right with her swipe about Mrs. Stratton paying with baked goods. He just wanted to work with his hands and had always enjoyed the thrill that brought him. Unfortunately, that didn't always pay the bills, and he was thankful to Peter for keeping him on track financially.

Ashlyn's offer was generous and he certainly could use a cash job. She was spot on in her assessment of Dan. Scott could assign him, along with Larry and Caleb, to her project and probably have it done in months. Although he hadn't assessed it yet, he'd visited Jean a few times to drop of Tina's homemade bread and he was familiar with the property. Still, the thought of working with someone who made his blood boil was less than thrilling.

What was it about the woman that pissed him off? As her face blazed in his mind, he contemplated. She certainly was a looker, with those long lashes, almond-shaped eyes, and full red lips. And her tight body was a runner's body, which he understood being a runner himself. Scowling, he realized he was annoyed because she was attractive. Attraction had no place in his world and he resented the small sparks of desire that had flitted in his chest when she'd approached him yesterday. Desire was something he no longer had the luxury of experiencing and he didn't relish the thought of being around a woman as viscerally stunning as Ashlyn Rivers.

Also, she was a pain in the ass. Growing up in Ardor Creek, Scott had never understood the brashness of city folk. He appreciated the small-town life and had no idea how someone as impetuous and bossy as Ashlyn would even begin to thrive in their rural environment. It would be a massive adjustment but the woman did seem to love a challenge. Smirking, he realized he might actually enjoy seeing her try to flourish in Ardor Creek. Hell, maybe she'd prove him wrong. And who was he to label someone as brash anyway? He certainly wasn't a ball of sunshine lately.

Double-clicking on the financial software program, he performed a quick analysis of the firm's cash flow. Yes, they really could use an all cash-up-front job. Cupping his chin, he crunched the numbers, waiting for Peter to arrive and confirm it was a terrible idea to take on Ashlyn's job...while, perhaps, secretly hoping his old friend told him the opposite so he could have an opportunity to observe the annoying woman attempt to shed her city ways and prosper in the quaint town he loved so dearly.

Chapter 5

Peter Stratford entered GDC, closing the door behind him as the bell chimed. Focusing his gaze on Carrie, he said, "Hey, Care Bear."

"Hey," she said, flashing him a brilliant smile. "You're just in time for some new gossip."

"Do tell," he said, leaning on his forearms and waggling his eyebrows. "Did you find a new lover to whisk you away now that Douchelord has moved to Colorado?"

Her features scrunched. "Still not sure I'm on board with that nickname but, yes, *Jeff* has settled half a country away with his new twenty-five-year-old wife and baby. I'm pretty sure I'll never hear from him again and couldn't be happier."

"He should be paying you child support and alimony, Carrie. It's the bare minimum he should be doing."

"I don't want it," she said, thrusting her chin in the air. "I never want to see him again. Some people say I'm in the wrong because I don't want him to have custody or see the boys, but I just don't give a damn. I'm happy to forego alimony and child support so he'll leave us the hell alone."

Peter's eyes darted over her face—those light-green eyes set below the endless red curls—and he felt the tug of emotion he always did around Carrie. It had been constant for so long, he'd given up on trying to purge it years ago. She was, and always would be, the one who got away. The fact that he'd all but pushed her into that scumbag Jeff Lawrence's arms fueled the rage that simmered in his gut. Man, he'd blown it, and, now, she had two kids and a shit-ton of baggage. Hell, their combined baggage would sink the Titanic a hundred times over. Pushing the musings aside, he smiled.

"So, you were going to give me the gossip on your new lover?"

She made a *pfft* sound and waved her hand. "Right. A divorced mom with seven and nine-year-old terror-inducing spawns. I'm not sure a lover would make it past the first fist-fight with those two." Biting her lip, she shrugged. "But they're so damn adorable, I think I'll keep them."

Chuckling, he nodded. "I think you're stuck with them, honey."

"But," she said, lifting a finger and leaning closer to whisper, "I think Scott might have the potential to have a thing for this hot new number who just moved into town from the city."

Peter's eyebrows lifted. "Really? He hasn't dated since Tina."

"I know." Her cheeks flushed, making her look exquisite as she excitedly carried on. "But she came in here yesterday and rattled him something fierce. Then, she tracked him down at the site over by Cyprus. I'm not sure he's ready for someone like Ashlyn, and I'm pretty damn happy about it."

"Well, hot damn." Straightening, he gave her a wink. "Let me assess. He's in his office?"

"Yep," she said, nodding. Sentiment entered her gaze as she stared up at him. "You look good, Peter. You've put back on all the weight you lost."

All the weight he'd lost the last time he'd shoved so many drugs in his system he'd ended up in rehab. For the last time. It had to be. He just didn't have the mental fortitude to survive another relapse.

"Thanks, Care Bear. One day at a time." With one last smile, he meandered through the office and knocked on Scott's glass door. His buddy waved him inside and he lowered into the chair.

"Well, I hear there's a hot new thing in town."

Sighing, Scott ran his hand over his face. "Sometimes I think I pay Carrie just to drive me insane. Is that in her job description?" He squinted at the ceiling.

Peter breathed a laugh. “She cares about you, Scott. We all do. It’s been almost six years. You’re going to have to grease the wheels eventually.”

“I have no interest in greasing the wheels,” he muttered.

“Right. I’ve seen the cookies and browser history on your computer. Porn Hub isn’t a bad choice but it won’t keep you warm at night.”

Scott’s lips flattened. “I’m searching for a legitimate reason as to why you’re accessing my browser history.”

Peter held up his hands. “Whoa, buddy, I’m on your side here. You did hire me as your accountant and give me ten percent of this lovely little company to keep tabs on your finances. That requires me to use your computer when you’re out on site visits sometimes. Don’t worry, I won’t tell. Although I didn’t realize you were into bondage. Pretty surprising for the saint of Ardor Creek, but we all have our hidden fetishes.”

“I’m trashing every computer in this place,” Scott said, glowering. “From now on, paper ledgers and Morse code.”

Chuckling, Peter shook his head. “Come on, man. Relax. You’re wound up as hell. I guess Carrie was right about Ashlyn.” Rubbing his chin, he pondered. “I like that name. Tell me about her. I heard she tracked you down at the Cyprus site.”

Scott updated him on Ashlyn and Peter calculated the influx of cash her job would add to the bottom line. “Honestly, Scott, I know you didn’t want to hire Dan, Larry, and Caleb out for a new job until we had more cash flow, but this is perfect. If she’s willing to pay up front, I don’t see a downside.”

“I’d have to work with her for the design and complete site inspections every few days. I’m not sure I’m up for that.”

“Why? Because she’s hot?”

“Because she’s annoying. And because we’ll be bidding on the Kingsley job soon.” Kingsley was a nearby town with a developer looking to build seven houses on a newly purchased plot of land. It was a perfect job for Scott’s firm and would be one of the most lucrative he’d ever procured.

"Yes, but if we win the bid we won't start building until early spring of next year. Plenty of time for your contractors to finish Ashlyn's renovation, right?"

"Yes," Scott gritted, a muscle ticking in his jaw.

"Man, you're all sorts of shook. I can't wait to meet this woman."

His friend just shot him a glare before exhaling a deep breath. "Whether I like it or not, I think I have to take this job. Do you agree?"

"I do," Peter said with a nod. "It's actually quite fortuitous timing. You should probably thank her for showing up out of the blue and offering to drop a wad of cash in your lap."

"I'm all set, but thanks." Standing, he ran his hand through his thick brown hair. "Want to grab lunch at the deli before you head back home to crunch numbers? I need to have a chat with Donna about running her mouth to city slickers."

"Oh, yeah," Peter said, rising and patting Scott on the back when he rounded the desk. "Wouldn't miss that conversation for the world. Lead the way, buddy."

Following him through the office, Peter waved at Carrie as she held the receiver to her ear, feeling his heartbeat accelerate when she smiled and waved back. Those little jolts of emotion reminded him that he'd once been able to love and process emotion, all those years ago before he'd become a broken mess that never quite fit back together. For that, he would always be thankful to Carrie Longwood, the only woman who'd ever stolen his heart.

Chapter 6

The run cleared Ashlyn's head and did wonders for her hangover. After a warm shower, she headed downstairs to see what shape the kitchen was in. The oven had seen better days but it was functional and she was ready to put it to good use. After her first trip to the local grocery store, which she was thrilled to see had a fantastic organic section, she returned home with overflowing bags. Unloading them on the counter, she fisted her hands on her hips and gave a nod. She was going to make Scott a gorgeous cake and give it to him while she ate a side of crow.

Several hours later, she observed the exquisite chocolate buttercream cake as it cooled. Grandma Jean had been a magnificent baker and had taught Ashlyn well. That, combined with her love of cooking, made her one hell of a whiz in the kitchen. Once the cake was cool enough to pack, she slid it into the Tupperware container and zipped up her hooded sweatshirt, ready to deliver it to Mr. Sexy-Surly Contractor. Approaching the front door, she drew it open...and found a stunned Scott Grillo on the other side.

"Uh, hi," she said, trying like hell not to drop the cake as she placed her free hand over her chest. "You scared the *crap* out of me."

"Sorry," he mumbled, his ever-present scowl situated on his handsome face. "I would've called but I don't have your number."

"Oh," she said, blinking rapidly. "Right. Well, this is certainly a surprise. If someone had told me an hour ago you'd show up at my doorstep asking for my number, I certainly would've guessed they had a few screws loose."

"I didn't exactly ask for your number."

"Well, you kinda did, in a roundabout way, but whatever."

"I absolutely did not."

His features were so stoic that she had to gulp down her laugh. Had this guy ever heard of fun, playful banter? Guess not. Geez. What did he do for fun? Knife throwing? Fold his socks? Watch grass grow? Snickering at her internal dialogue, she shrugged. "Okay, you win. I probably shouldn't argue with you since I was about to bring you this cake."

His eyes darted to the Tupperware. "You made me a cake?"

"Yep," she said, lifting the container. "I was all ready to apologize and tell you I was sorry for being so insistent. It's a habit from my former job. And, honestly, I've always been a tunnel-vision kind of person. Once I decide on something, I won't stop until I accomplish it. It's annoying but it also produces amazing results."

"It is annoying," he muttered. He must've noticed her fallen expression because he gestured with his hand. "It's also pretty admirable and says a lot about your fortitude. So, I guess I could also apologize for being so short with you. Carrie says I'm gruff sometimes."

"Sometimes?"

He shot her a droll look.

"Okay, okay, we were doing so well. Let's not ruin it." Waving him inside, she closed the door when he stepped in. "Are you here to do the survey?"

"I'm considering it."

"Sweet. Come to the kitchen and have some cake. I'm not above bribery." She sauntered into the kitchen, hoping he would follow, and set the container on the island. Sure enough, he appeared and she directed him to sit on one of the stools. "Here," she said, sliding out the cake and locating the cutter in a nearby drawer. "You're going to love this."

"I don't like chocolate."

Ashlyn looked at him like he had five heads. "Who in the world doesn't like chocolate?"

"Me."

A laugh escaped her throat as she observed his sullen expression. "Well, you're going to like *this* chocolate. It's laced with buttercream. Let's make a bet. If you like it, you'll take the job. If you hate it, I'll leave you alone forever."

He adjusted his glasses as he studied her. "Deal."

Jumping into action, she located two plates and forks. Lowering onto the stool beside him, she cut them both a piece.

"You're going to eat a piece of the apology cake you baked for me?"

She shrugged. "Might as well since you don't like chocolate. Don't want it to go to waste if you hate it. Can't have it both ways, Scott." His response was that now-familiar acerbic stare, so she forged ahead. Picking up her fork, she gave him a cheeky grin. "Dig in."

He grasped the fork like it was the leg of a venomous spider while she took a bite, deciding he could win a contest for "Slowest Eater in the World." Chewing the delicious morsel, she was resolved that anyone who didn't like it had malfunctioning taste buds.

His strong jaw worked as he chewed the piece and Ashlyn squirmed on the stool, trying to discern if he like it. "Well?" she asked after a small eternity.

Those melted brown eyes locked onto hers. "It's creamy."

Well, he was certainly no Bill Shakespeare. Scott Grillo was a man of few words if she'd ever met one. "Creamy and...?"

"It's good," he said, sticking his fork into the cake to pluck off another bite. Ashlyn felt like she'd won a goddamn Olympic medal.

"Yeah?"

Nodding, he lifted his gaze to hers again. There was a speck of cake on his full bottom lip and she thought she saw the barest hint of a smile there.

"Holy shit. You're going to renovate my house," she said, sliding a napkin toward him.

He wiped his lips and set the napkin on the counter. "Ms. Rivers, I'm going to renovate your house."

"Yippee!" Jumping from the stool, she pumped her fists in the air a few times while he chuckled. The sound was low and deep, thus confirming the man did, indeed, possess the ability to laugh. Go figure.

"Okay, eat up," she said, sitting back down. "Once we're done, I'll give you the grand tour."

A few minutes later, she showed Scott around as he took meticulous notes. He agreed with her assessments about which rooms needed renovation, which pleased her since she'd mostly lived in apartments in the city.

"Did you have the car in the city?" he asked.

"Yeah," she said, leading him to the attic entrance. "I found a garage where I paid a couple of hundred bucks a month to park it. I needed it to visit Grandma and my parents in New Jersey."

Nodding, he stared at the ceiling entrance with the dangling string. "Want to show me the attic?"

"Yes," she said, grasping the string and tugging. The compartment fell open and she unfolded the stairs. "I'm not going to renovate up here because I want to keep the originality of the space for the ghost tour but you've got to see this." Excitement grew as she trailed up the stairs.

Once they were in the dim attic, Ashlyn illuminated the flashlight app on her phone. "Get a load of that," she almost whispered, shining it on the dusty wooden rocking chair.

"Is that the chair where they found Sally Pickens?" he asked, eyes widening.

"One and the same. How cool is that? Grandma could never get rid of it. Said this house was always Sally's as much as it was hers. I swear, I think she used to speak to her when she was lonely."

Scott's features constricted. "You know that sounds insane."

"You don't believe in ghosts?"

"No."

Ashlyn's eyes darted over his face, realizing this man had more ghosts than anyone she'd probably ever encountered. "Maybe they believe in you."

His features resumed their emotionless mask, frustrating Ashlyn as she realized she'd blown the goodwill that had built over the last half hour. *Way to go, Rivers.*

"What was that?"

"Oh," she said, waving a hand. "I must've said that out loud. I talk to myself. A lot. It drove my ex crazy." Something flashed in his eyes at the word "ex" and it looked a lot like curiosity. Hmmm, *that* was interesting. "Anyway," she continued, "I also conduct a lot of self-pep-talks. They motivate me. What can I say?"

When he remained silent, she shrugged. "Okay, then. I think I've shown you everything. Let me pack up the cake so you can take it with you." After maneuvering down the stairs and closing up the attic entrance, she slid the cake in the Tupperware.

"You can keep it if you want. After all, you ate half of it."

"I ate *one* piece and now I realize I'll never live that down," she said, flashing a smile. "Here, I'll carry it to your car since you're holding the notes." They trailed outside, down the porch steps, stopping beside the driver's side door of his SUV. He threw the notepad in the front seat and Ashlyn extended the container. "Enjoy and maybe take it to the office tomorrow. I bet Carrie would love a piece."

"I will," he said, grasping it and holding it to his chest. Standing still, he contemplated her, making her slightly uncomfortable.

"Thank you, Scott," she said, taking a step back, indicating he was free to go. "I really appreciate you taking on this job."

"Thanks for paying up front," he said with a tilt of his head. "I'll have a quote for you by tomorrow afternoon."

"Pro tip? Quote high, because I'm a killer negotiator."

His lips formed a grin. "If you were that great, you wouldn't tell me that."

"Oh, buddy, you have no idea." She patted his shoulder. "I'm just trying to be nice before I decimate you."

When he still didn't budge, she lifted her shoulders. "Do you want to ask me something, Scott?"

Sighing, his gaze fell to the cake before lifting back to hers. "Did you bake this for me because you found out what happened to my family?"

The question shocked her for some reason. It seemed like an accusation although there wasn't any harshness in his tone. "I...uh, well..." Running her hand through her hair, she puffed a breath through her lips. "That might have had something to do with it but

I also truly wanted to apologize. I'm new in town and don't want to make enemies. I'd really like us to be friends, Scott. I wasn't above eating a little crow to make that happen."

He nodded, appearing to process her answer.

"I'm so sorry about what happened—"

Holding up a hand, he shook his head. "I don't want to discuss it."

"Okay," she said, crossing her arms over her chest. "Well, you brought it up."

Lips pursed, he glanced down. "You were just someone who didn't know. It was nice, for just a minute, to be around someone who didn't know. That's all."

Realization swamped her as she comprehended that his life was defined by this one incident. The threads of the consequences of that accident dictated everything in his existence. "I can still be that person, Scott. Consider it forgotten." Sliding her thumb and forefinger over her lips, she mimicked zipping them shut and throwing away the key. "From now on, I'll just be your annoying client and you'll be my contractor. Scott and Ashlyn with no pasts, only the future. What do you say?"

Those full lips twitched. "It sounds nice, actually."

"Great. It's settled then. Get me the quote and come ready for battle because I'm going to shred it."

He'd now broken into a full-blown smile, causing her legs to turn to jelly as her rapidly beating heart pulsed blood through her veins. Man, he was *hot* and her reaction to him was visceral. "Can't wait, Ashlyn."

As he folded into the car, the sound of her name spoken in his silken tone all but made her mouth water. Shutting the door, he gave her a wave, which she returned before watching him drive off. Swallowing thickly, she slid her hands in the back pockets of her jeans, frozen in place as the image of his perfect smile lingered.

"Oh, girl," she muttered, "you are in serious trouble."

Expelling a sigh, she trudged back to the house, realizing she was already halfway smitten with her handsome new contractor.

Chapter 7

Scott's fingers ticked away at the keyboard as he prepared Ashlyn's quote. Tongue situated between his teeth, he meticulously plugged in the numbers as Peter sauntered in and slid into the seat in front of his desk. Straightening in his chair, Scott thrust his fingers through his hair as he expelled a deep breath.

"Eighty-five thousand and change," he said.

Peter gave a low whistle. "For two bathrooms, a kitchen, a den, and a front porch? Seems steep."

"It is," he said, wondering if he was being an ass for inflating the numbers. "The job's closer to seventy thousand but she told me to come in high because she wants to negotiate. Is this too much? I feel like a slumlord or a gangster or something."

"You? A gangster? No way, buddy," Peter said, chuckling as he unwrapped one of the peppermints on Scott's desk and threw it in his mouth. "The quote's good. It'll give her room to negotiate and still net you some cash. You're getting the hang of this, man."

"Yeah, I still hate this part of the business. Speaking of, did you finish the business plan for the Kingsley quote?"

"Emailed it to you twenty minutes ago."

Checking his email, Scott double-clicked and brought up the document. He and Peter spent the next hour discussing it and going over the details. "This is great. You're really earning that ten percent cut."

"Thanks," he said, grinning. "I miss the number crunching so it's fun for me. Being a broker was way more exciting than being a small-town accountant."

"Are you bored here?"

Peter shrugged. "I don't know. Maybe. Sometimes the pull of the big city is so strong, I feel it in my bones. But I can't go back there. It's just not a healthy environment for me."

Scott regarded him, understanding how many changes his friend had made to save his own life. "I'm proud of you. You worked hard to reclaim your life. It's a huge accomplishment."

Scoffing, he lifted his shoulders. "And now, I live in my childhood home with my ailing mother. A real success story."

"Hey, I know she loves having you home and it's important to spend time with our parents. You never know when they're going to go."

Peter nodded, acknowledging that Scott's parents had both passed over ten years ago. "Very true."

"And your accounting business is growing. I think you service over half the business owners in town. Like I've said before, whenever you're ready to stop working out of your home office, I can build you an office here. It would be a nice addition to the space."

"Maybe one day. Taking on too much shit is what got me in trouble in the first place. My sponsors all tell me to take it easy. One day at a time and all that jazz. So, that's what I'm doing. The one stock portfolio I didn't blow on drugs and hookers is doing quite well which makes me a hell of a lot luckier than most addicts."

Scott nodded. "I assume 'taking it slow' means no dating."

"Yeah, man. I've got nothing to offer any woman. Just a busted up nose from too much coke and a crap ton of mistakes."

"Carrie knew you before you made those mistakes."

His dark eyebrow arched. "Carrie has two sons who need a father figure, not a washed-up druggie. And, honestly man, I messed that up years ago. Since she has the biggest heart in the world, she forgave me, which I'll always be grateful for. But it will always be between us—the memories of the person I used to be. She deserves better."

"Maybe she deserves the person you've become."

With a *pfft*, he waved his hand and straightened in the chair. "This is a pointless discussion. And who are you to give advice anyway? Come find me when *you* start dating again. Then we'll talk."

As if on cue, the image of Ashlyn's stunning face flitted through Scott's mind. Feeling his muscles tense, he remembered those dark green eyes as she stared up at him with compassion. Her offer to move forward without rehashing the past had moved something in him. She seemed to understand the burden that came with discussing those tragic events with almost everyone he came into contact with. In a small town, people felt that everyone's business was open game. Although he knew they meant well, he always hated talking about the accident. Ashlyn had freed him from that burden, creating anticipation of their future interactions. What would it be like to just be friends with someone without having them gaze upon you with pity or sadness? He had no idea and was actually looking forward to finding out.

"Well, hot damn," Peter said, eyes lit with excitement. "Someone's got a little crush."

Scott rolled his eyes. "I do not. She's just not quite as annoying as I thought. That's all."

"Well, for you, that's one step from true love." Scott scowled. "Oh, yeah, this is awesome. I need to meet this woman stat. I was thinking about having a few people over on Saturday. It's going to be nice and it will give me a reason to clean the grill. What do you say? You can bring her as your date."

"No."

Chuckling, Peter stood. "Okay, I'll have Carrie invite her, then. Show up or don't, but it should be fun. I know you remember somewhere in the back of that stubborn head of yours what fun is. Catch you later." With a salute, he exited the office.

"I remember what fun is," Scott mumbled, absently clicking the mouse as he saved the various open documents. Once they were all closed, he removed his glasses and ran his hands over his face, admitting the lie. Fun had exited his life long ago, along with so many other things.

Feeling his lips quirk, he corrected himself, realizing the sentiment wasn't exactly true. He'd had fun with Ashlyn yesterday as they'd sat together and toured the house, chatting amicably as if they'd known each other for years. Their comradery had come easily, along with the banter that he found quite charming.

Lost in yesterday's memories, he wondered why the feelings they generated scared the hell out of him.

Chapter 8

Ashlyn's phone chimed from her back pocket as she sowed the dirt with the tiny hoe. She was determined to plant a thriving garden in her backyard and had already tilled most of the area. Wiping sweat from her brow, she checked the caller ID. Grinning, she answered, putting the phone on speaker and setting it down as she resumed her actions with the hoe.

"Hello, Mr. Grillo. How are you today?"

"Fine," his deep voice chimed through the phone. "You?"

"Good. Just working on my garden. Did you prepare the quote?"

"I did. Ready and waiting for you to shred."

"You learn quickly, young Jedi," she teased.

Chuckling, he said, "Well, I figured you might want to negotiate in person. If so, we can meet over dinner at the pub if you like. I'll be free any time after five-thirty."

"That would rock actually," she said, plopping down on her butt and lifting her phone closer. "I've been wanting to try some places in town."

"Great. Want to meet there at six?"

"Sure," she said, feeling her eyes narrow. "I don't know a lot about small towns, but will this set tongues wagging? Us having dinner together? Will people think it's a date?"

"One thing everyone in this town understands is that I have no interest in dating."

Huh. For some reason, that statement hit her straight in the solar plexus, causing her to rub her chest. "All right, then. Six o'clock it is. Can't wait to show you my skills."

His laugh washed over her. "Bring it on. See you later."

The phone clicked and she rested her arms on her knees, staring ahead as she digested the conversation. "Well, Rivers, at least he's not leading you on. Better than the alternative." Not wanting to waste one second thinking of Robert, she finished the section and stood, wiping her hands on her butt.

After a refreshing shower, she flicked through the clothes in the closet, wondering what to wear. Everything had now been moved from Manhattan, thanks to the movers who'd shown up this morning, and the final month's rent had been paid on her apartment. All her ties to the city were essentially cut. It was a bit overwhelming and she took some deep breaths to steady herself as she perused the closet.

Deciding on jeans, ankle boots, and a silky top, she made sure her makeup looked presentable and straightened her hair. It fell black and smooth past her shoulders as she studied her reflection. "You've still got it, Rivers. Screw him." Not wanting to give Robert any more of her energy, she shrugged on her light jacket and drove into town.

Finding an open spot, she parked against the sidewalk and headed into the bar. It was half-full and she sat at one of the high top tables set for two. A waitress walked over, teeth flashing as she asked, "Want a drink, sweetheart?"

"Sure do. Vodka soda, please."

"Sure thing," the woman said, a sparkle in her eyes. "You're Ashlyn Rivers, right? Scott stopped by earlier and told us you were meeting him here. A bunch of us knew your grandma and were really fond of her. So sorry for your loss."

"Thank you."

"When Scott stopped by he was clear y'all were having a business meeting and not a date, so we're all taking bets on how much he actually *wishes* it was a date."

Ashlyn bit her lip. "Oh, crap. I don't think he'll like that."

"Don't worry, city girl. We know how to handle him. My name's Terry. I'll grab your drink and Scott's, too, since he only ever drinks Arnold Palmers."

Ashlyn wondered if he didn't drink because his family had been killed by a drunk driver.

"Yep, you got it," Terry said, sliding the pen behind her ear. "Not one drink since the accident. If you ask me, it might do him good to get plastered, just for a night, but he's pretty set on it. Can't say I blame him, of course."

"Of course," she said as her lips formed a sympathetic smile. "It's definitely not a date, Terry."

"Oh, I know it's not. For now." Terry gave a wink before turning to walk away. "Be back with that drink in a minute."

Left alone with her tap water, Ashlyn studied the menu until Scott appeared beside her. "Hey," he said, sliding into the seat. "Sorry, I'm a few minutes late. Got stuck on a call with a client. Did Terry stop by?"

"Yep. I ordered a drink and she's going to bring you the usual."

Nodding, he glanced at the menu. "How long did it take for her to tell you they were going to gossip about us all night?"

"About thirty seconds," Ashlyn said, laughing.

"Sounds about right." Pointing to the menu, he said, "The nachos are really good. Want to share?"

"Sure. I'll just run an extra mile or two tomorrow."

Sitting back, he studied her. "Do you run every morning?"

"Five days a week." Terry appeared, dropping off the drink as she greeted Scott. Ashlyn squeezed the lime into the glass, and he placed the nacho order before Terry scampered away. "Anyway, running clears my head and keeps me focused."

"I enjoy running too. Got some new orthotics that should help my shin splints. I should probably take it easy but I just can't find that runner's high anywhere else."

"I get it," she said, sipping from the tiny red straw. "There's definitely nothing like it. Is there a runner's club here? I enjoyed the one I joined in Manhattan. If not, maybe we could run together sometime and also think about starting one."

"Yeah, I'm not really great with group activities."

Ashlyn arched a brow. "Because they require you to stop scowling for longer than ten seconds?"

"Ha. Ha," he said, drawing out the words. "I don't scowl. I'm just always contemplating something really important."

She huffed a laugh. "Okay."

That elicited a twitch of his lips, which made her insides melt. He was really charming when he relaxed a bit. "I can try running with you one morning. I guess it wouldn't kill me."

"Sweet. We'll pick a date. In the meantime, what else should I order? If I'm going to overload on calories, might as well go for the gold."

She decided on a turkey club with fries and he ordered the glazed salmon with veggies. The meal was fantastic and Ashlyn sighed as she downed the last fry. "Definitely gonna need two or three extra miles after that feast but it was worth it. And you were right about the nachos. I loved the spicy salsa. Yum."

"You two want dessert?" Terry asked, appearing beside the table and clearing their plates.

"None for me," Ashlyn said, resting her hands over her abdomen. "I'm about to bust wide open."

"I'm good," Scott said. "We're going to discuss Ms. Rivers' quote but let us know if you need the table."

"It's yours for however long you want it, honey," Terry said, trailing away.

"Do you want another drink?" he asked, pointing at the empty vodka soda.

"Nice try but I'll be wasted if I have more than two and I need to retain my skills." She waggled her eyebrows.

"All right, then, let's get to it." Extracting a manilla folder from his briefcase, he flipped it open and pulled out the quote. Sliding it across the table, he pointed with his finger. "Everything is summarized here on page one and then there's a detailed breakdown for each section."

Ashlyn whistled. "Eighty-five thousand. The idea here is for me to renovate my home, not to render me homeless."

Lifting his hands, he shrugged. "You said to come in high."

"Fair enough," she murmured, dragging her finger over the quote. "Okay, let's start crunching these numbers." Pulling a pen from her bag and pulling up the calculator app on her phone, she began scribbling. Each section was meticulously debated as she flipped through each page of the quote.

"It does *not* cost five thousand dollars to install a separate tub in the second bedroom."

"I have to rework the plumbing to facilitate that. The plumber I work with, John Rollins, is fantastic but he's not cheap. You can hire a different plumber but I trust John implicitly and he's worth the price tag."

"Then you can remove several hours of labor on the first bathroom. I'm keeping the shower and tub combination in that one so it should only cost half since you don't have to rework the plumbing."

The corner of his lips curved. "I could come down on the first bathroom."

"You're damn right you can. And in the kitchen you charged me for the counters and the island but, technically, they both fall under the 'counter' category, so we can cut there..." Trailing off, she indicated the note and continued through the pages, slashing his numbers along the way.

"There," she said, half an hour later, lifting her head triumphantly as she beamed. "Sixty-five thousand and change. I think that's good."

Scott's eyes narrowed. "I won't do it for less than seventy thousand."

"I'm not agreeing to anything with a seven in front of it, sorry." Lifting her cup of water, she leaned forward. "Sixty-nine thousand flat and we're good to go."

Scott mulled the offer as she waited with bated breath.

Lifting his Arnold Palmer, he clinked it with her glass. "Sixty-nine thousand flat. Ms. Rivers, you have yourself a deal."

Thrilled at her handiwork, she smiled as Terry approached. "What are we celebrating?"

"Sixty-nine on the dot," Ashlyn said, so tickled she almost giggled.

"Well," Terry said, lifting a brow. "Never thought I'd find you two discussing sixty-nines. Maybe you do need another drink, honey." She winked at Ashlyn.

"We're discussing her quote, which we've agreed will land at sixty-nine thousand *dollars*," Scott said, annoyed.

"Uh-huh," Terry said, glancing back and forth between them. "Well, I say that deserves one on the house. I'll grab you both another round and leave the check here for whenever you're ready." Placing the check on the table, she headed to the bar as Ashlyn smiled.

"Guess I'm having one more vodka soda after all." Picking up the tab, she reached for her purse.

"I've got it," Scott said, snatching it from her hand.

"I can split it with you."

"I'll write it off," he said, throwing his card over the check. It shouldn't have made her all warm and fuzzy that he wanted to pay for what he clearly saw as a business dinner, but damn if it didn't make her insides tingle anyway.

"Thank you," she said, lifting the fresh drink Terry dropped off. "This has been fun."

"It has," he said, knocking her glass with his before taking a sip. "I didn't hate negotiating with you nearly as much as I thought I would."

Ashlyn rolled her eyes. "You're a real master at compliments there, Scott."

Laughing, he shrugged. "I'm pretty rusty on compliments and fun and a whole bunch of other stuff according to my business partner. Cut me some slack and I'll try to do better."

"Are you going to be able to put up with your annoying new client?" She pointed both thumbs at her chest. "I might drive you nuts."

"Eh, you're not as terrible as I thought. More Darth Maul than Darth Vader."

"I'd be pissed at that except I'm absolutely thrilled by the Star Wars reference, so I'll let it lie. I'm a huge fan."

"I figured from your Jedi comment. I enjoy it too. I might have subscribed to Disney Plus solely for The Mandalorian." He gave a sheepish grin.

"No shame in that game. I'm here for it."

They finished their drinks and headed out into the cool night.

"Thanks so much for dinner," she said, smiling up at him as they stood beside her car.

"You're welcome. Thanks for taking it easy on me. I could've gone down to sixty-five."

Her shoulders lifted. "I could've done seventy-five so it looks like we both won. Should I text you about grabbing that jog one day this week?"

"Sure. I have an early site visit tomorrow morning, which isn't the norm but can't be avoided. I'm open later in the week though."

"Sweet. I'll reach out to set a date. Have a good night."

He followed her around to the driver's side door and reached for the handle, drawing it open. "Have a good night." Ashlyn's heart melted at the chivalrous gesture. Once inside, he closed the door and hopped back on the sidewalk, standing still and giving a wave before she drove away.

When she arrived home, she trailed inside, making her way to the bathroom and staring at her reflection. Her cheeks were flushed but that was probably from the vodka. Staring into her dark green orbs, she whispered, "Liar."

There was only one explanation for the warmth coursing through her body and his name was Scott Grillo. Determined not to lie to herself, she acknowledged her attraction and locked it away. Self-deception had led her down a disastrous path with Robert and she wouldn't repeat the same mistakes. Admitting the truth was fine. There was nothing illegal about having a crush on an intelligent, handsome man. The fact that he didn't want her back and only saw her as a client? Even better.

Realizing that was yet another lie, Ashlyn shut down the inner conversation and told herself to go to bed.

Chapter 9

The next morning, Ashlyn sat at the round kitchen table going over her finances as she sipped coffee. Now that she no longer had to pay rent, and thanks to excellent self-management of her stock options and savings, she calculated she could comfortably live without a steady income for almost two years, even with the renovation. Of course, she wouldn't rest on her laurels that long. She'd always possessed a drive and motivation that led her to push herself far past where others would claim exhaustion. It's what had led to her stunning sales success and what had allowed her to build up her impressive financial portfolio.

But it had also been draining. As a woman in the male-dominated field of biotech pharmaceutical sales—much different than the more widely-known prescription salespeople—she'd scraped and clawed to achieve the number one spot each year. Although it had been financially and personally rewarding, it had detracted from other aspects of her life. If she hadn't been so focused on achieving success, she might've realized how badly her relationship had deteriorated. Unfortunately, she'd missed the signs—or perhaps just ignored them—causing her well-crafted life to crumble.

The dissolution of her relationship also spurred her to realize that the break-neck corporate career she'd chosen didn't make her happy. Each success led to one moment of elation followed by a quick return to the arduous ten-hour workdays and stuffy physician dinners she hated. When Jean bequeathed her the house, Ashlyn saw it as an opportunity to make a clean break and free herself from the self-imposed prison she'd created. Perhaps her grandma had understood it would prompt her to make some much-needed changes.

"You always knew me best," she said, glancing around the house, hoping Jean could hear her, wherever she was in the universe. "Thank you, Grandma. I'm going to make better choices this time. I promise."

A clatter sounded upstairs, causing Ashlyn to jump. Rising from the chair, she tentatively headed up the stairs searching for what could've made the sound. Entering the bathroom at the top of the stairs, she noticed the hand soap now sat in the sink, somehow lodged from the spot where it usually sat beside the faucet.

"Did you knock this over, Grandma?" she murmured, setting the soap back where it belonged. "Or maybe Sally Pickens?" Rubbing her arms to control her slight shiver, she stared at the ceiling, ears perked as she listed to the attic above. Tiny hairs stood along her arms as she heard the slight creaking sound, back and forth, as if someone was rocking in the chair. Straining further, she realized it was most likely coming from the vent that sat above the bathroom window. Although the weather had been nice for late-March, Ashlyn had been running the heat in the mornings and evenings.

"Just the heat, Ashlyn," she said, struggling to regulate her now elevated breathing. "Just the heat." Heading back downstairs, she resumed working on her computer.

Her phone dinged and lit up atop the table and she read the text from her previous neighbor.

Sarah: Hey, Ashlyn. Hope you're settled in BFE! Just kidding. Robert showed up here asking if I knew your new address. I think he was trying to get it from the movers too. I made sure they didn't divulge anything. Just wanted to let you know. Ping me when you visit the city and we'll grab sushi.

Sighing, Ashlyn returned a text.

Ashlyn: Sorry he bothered you. I have him blocked. EVERYWHERE. Hopefully, I'll never see his worthless ass again. Will definitely reach out when I visit. Miss you and take care! Xoxo

Resuming her work, Ashlyn spent some time looking at various food trucks for sale. The inventory wasn't great but there were some possibilities. She could also purchase a truck and recommission it for food service. Clicking through the listings, she scowled when her phone rang, showing an unknown number. Lifting it, she swiped her finger across the screen and said, "Hello?"

"Don't hang up," Robert's deep voice chimed. "I'm using a friend's phone since you blocked me. I need to see you, Ashlyn."

Rolling her eyes, she struggled not to crush the phone into tiny bits. "Lose my number. Don't *ever* call me again. It's over, Robert."

"She meant nothing to me, Ash, don't you get it? You were just working so much and I was lonely. You're blaming me for everything, and I'm so damn sorry, but we both are responsible for what happened."

Scoffing, she rested her head in her hand, disbelief coursing through her veins. "*I'm* responsible for you sticking your dick into someone else's vagina? Don't think so, buddy. Good try."

"Ashlyn—"

"I mean it, Robert. This had better be the last time I ever hear your voice. Leave me the hell alone and don't ever call or text me again. If I so much as see a damn carrier pigeon from you, I'll file a restraining order. Got it? Goodbye."

Clicking off the phone, she threw it on the table and speared her fingers through her hair, giving a loud groan. The phone rang again and she picked it up and yelled, "You son of a bitch—"

"Whoa," Carrie's voice chimed from the other end. "Did we get off on *that* bad of a foot?"

Glancing at the screen, Ashlyn noticed the caller ID said *Grillo Design and Construction*. Huffing a breath, she flopped back in her seat. "Sorry, Carrie. Bad timing. I thought you were someone else."

"Well, I would hope so. I was sure I'd built up some goodwill since I gave you the scoop on how to track down Scott."

Chuckling, she nodded. "You did. I'm really sorry. Crazy morning over here. What's up?"

"I'm calling to discuss the schedule with you, now that you and Scott have agreed on the numbers."

"Awesome. Let's do it."

Scott would spend the next month designing the renovations and obtaining the proper permits. Dan, Larry, and Caleb would be assigned to the job and begin the renovation in late-April. They would start with the bathrooms, then renovate the fireplace, den and kitchen before completing the porch. Overall, they would be finished in early September, giving Ashlyn time to prepare for the haunted homes tour.

"The timetable is perfect, Carrie. Thanks so much. I guess this means I have to cut you a check."

"Sure does, honey. Want to bring it by? I'm always here from nine to three."

"I'll get a cashier's check later today and stop by." Biting her lip, she asked, "Is Scott in the office today?"

"He's in and out, as usual."

"Cool. Just wondering."

"Uh-huh." Ashlyn could envision her smile on the other side of the phone. "While I've got you, my friend Peter is having a backyard barbeque on Saturday. Since it's been so warm, he wants to break out his grill. He asked me to invite you."

"Oh," Ashlyn said, considering. "That's really nice. Peter Stratford?"

"One and the same. He and I would both really like you to come. You can meet some of the locals, although you've already charmed Terry. She mentioned how much she enjoyed meeting you at the pub. Come around two o'clock on Saturday. I'll text you so you have the address."

"Can't wait. Thank you, Carrie."

"Sure thing. See you later, honey."

Holding the phone to her chest, Ashlyn smiled, already feeling a connection with Carrie. Would Scott be at the barbeque? Probably. Would he find it weird that she was there? Maybe, but there was no doubt he would know she was invited. She'd enjoyed their dinner and realized she wanted to see him again before they had to be in a social setting. It made sense so they could continue building their comradery.

"Or maybe you just want to see him again because he's so damn hot," she mumbled.

Sighing, she opened the message tab and shot him a text.

Ashlyn: Hi. It's your favorite client. Want to grab that jog Friday morning?

Waiting with bated breath as the text bubble appeared, she sipped her lukewarm coffee.

Scott: Sure. Want to meet in front of GDC at seven? Or is that too early?

Ashlyn: Works for me. I'm pretty competitive. Come ready to eat my dust.

Scott: Quaking in my boots. See you then.

Biting her lip to contain her smile, Ashlyn conjured up images of Scott all hot and sweaty from a nice, long run.

"Down girl. You made a celibacy pact, remember? And he's not interested anyway."

Closing her laptop, she headed up the stairs to shower, surprised at how excited she was for the upcoming jog. Even though she'd vowed to be celibate, her eyes worked just fine and she was ready to put them to good use while she ran alongside her sexy contractor.

Chapter 10

As Scott parked his car in front of GDC Friday morning, he admitted he was excited to see Ashlyn. When he'd gotten her text asking him for the jog, he'd smiled like an idiot at the phone, causing Carrie to shoot him a knowing glance. He'd told her to mind her business which resulted in a laugh from the woman who never took his sour attitude seriously.

After locking the car, he stuffed his keys inside his pocket and stretched as her sedan ambled down the street. When Ashlyn exited the car, his heart jolted in his chest, coursing blood through every vein in his body. Annoyed, he hoped he wasn't tenting his damn running shorts with the erection that was now fully forming.

The smooth skin of her stomach was exposed between her sports bra and tiny shorts. Green and pink sneakers completed her attire under sleek, silky legs. Scott's mouth was suddenly flooded with saliva, which pooled in the back of his throat as she approached. Man, she was *gorgeous.*

"You're not cold?" he asked, hating his gruff tone but suddenly unable to control his voice.

Her gaze trailed down her body before locking with his. "I'm fine. The chill motivates me to run faster and build up a sweat. And you're not wearing a sweatshirt."

No, but he was at least covered by his t-shirt and shorts. He noticed a mole a few inches from her navel and realized he was staring. Telling himself not to be a creep, he pointed to the edge of the road. "I figured we'd head down Main Street, around town, and then back by the clock before finishing. There's a meadow behind the office where we can stretch afterward."

"Great. I stretched at home so I'm ready," she said, beaming. "Let's do it."

They set off on their inaugural run, setting a brisk pace that thankfully had Scott's heart beating from exertion instead of desire. They chatted every few minutes about safe and general topics: her Grandma Jean, their favorite hobbies (karaoke for Ashlyn and golf for Scott), and her move to Ardor Creek.

"How are you liking the town so far, city girl?" he teased as he ran alongside her.

"I really like it." Surprise laced her tone. "I wasn't sure I would but I needed a change. It was scary to upend my entire life but opportunities to start over don't come along often and I knew I'd regret it if I didn't seize the moment."

"I admire you," he said, feeling a deep swell of veneration for her ability to change and adapt so quickly. "Not all of us are equipped with the ability to change. Sometimes people get stuck and if you're stuck long enough you just accept your circumstances."

Those deep green eyes lifted to his, filled with sympathy. "I hear that," she said, huffing slightly as she ran. "I really do, Scott, but sometimes you have to find a way to get unstuck. Believe me, it wasn't easy to leave everything I've known for years. But I knew happiness was waiting on the other side if I was brave enough to reach for it. Well, I hope it is, at least. So far, so good."

Scott pondered everything he'd discovered about Ashlyn so far. From her dogged pursuit of his contracting services to her strength and fortitude in reshaping her life. Wondering if he'd ever met anyone as scrappy and resilient, he felt his lips curve. She was a fighter and he'd given up on fighting so long ago. Perhaps being near her—with that determined, fiery personality—would inspire him to try again. Try for what? He wasn't quite sure, but for the first time in so long, he felt the sparks of excitement and anticipation deep within. He'd all but written off his future, choosing to live day by day in the world he'd fashioned for himself, but if this woman could start over from scratch, could he possibly do the same?

"Is that the field you mentioned where we could stretch?" she asked as they rounded the corner that led back to his office.

"Yep. Race you there."

Laughing, she bolted into a sprint. He let her pull ahead before tearing past her and stopping before the wooden fence. Resting his hands on his knees, he gulped air into his lungs.

"That was some sprint," she said, struggling to catch her breath. "My water's in the car but my legs feel like jelly."

"Be right back." Jogging to the back door of his office, he unlocked it and ran inside, grabbing two bottles of water before returning to the meadow.

"You're a saint," she said, grabbing the bottle and chugging half before wiping her arm over her mouth. "That was an awesome run. I enjoy running with other people much more than alone. I usually listen to podcasts while I jog but talking to someone else is much better."

"It was fun," he said, leaning against the fence as he stretched his leg behind his back. "We should do it again."

"So, I didn't drive you crazy?"

Chuckling, he bent forward, legs outstretched as he placed his palms on the ground. "You're officially no longer my annoying client. I think we might just be neighbors who are becoming friends."

"Are we neighbors?" she teased. "I have no idea where you live."

"Only about a mile from here, down Elm Street. I can walk on nice days but usually drive because I need the car for site visits."

Nodding, she plopped to the ground and crossed one leg over the other, using her arm for leverage as she twisted and stretched. He did the same, reaching down to massage his shins.

"Shin splints?"

"Yeah. I got new orthotics and they're pretty good but I'm resigned to the fact that I'll always have some residual pain."

Her gaze glided over his legs before she shimmied closer. "My friend Sarah had an awesome doctor in the city who showed her this technique to relieve her shin pain. We used to jog together and she said it was heaven. Want me to show you?" She lifted her hands, rotating them.

Scott's throat bobbed as he swallowed. Did he want her to touch his sweaty skin with those hands with cute red fingernails at the tips? Fuck yes. Was that a good idea? Definitely not. "I, uh, you don't have to..."

"Oh," she said as understanding flooded her expression. "I didn't even think. I swear that wasn't a come-on or whatever. Man, I'm such an idiot. Sorry." She shook her head, remorse and pity entering those stunning eyes.

If there was one thing Scott hated, it was pity. During his sessions with his therapist after the accident, his one complaint had been how much people insisted on treating him with kid gloves. Seeing it in Ashlyn spurred anger deep within since he wanted so badly to connect with someone who didn't make everything about his past.

"Go ahead," he said, gesturing with his head toward his legs. "Show me."

Her eyes widened. "Are you sure?"

Nodding, he clenched his teeth as she placed her hands over his shin. Digging the heels of both hands on either side of the bone, she pushed, the pulsing sensation sending sparks of pleasure through his frame. Not only because it relieved the tension from the splints but because her skin was so damn soft against the prickly hairs.

"The heels of your hands work better than your fingers because they create a wider base. I used to do this for Sarah after we jogged sometimes. She was a physical therapist and never had a problem with me touching her." A nervous chuckle escaped her lips.

Scott sure as hell didn't mind having her touch him either. No, he was pretty sure that sometime over the last thirty seconds he'd exited Earth and entered heaven. Her hands circled his leg, up and down, sending erotic images through his mind about having them massage another place on his straining body. Finishing with the first leg, she trailed her hands to the other, digging her heels in the flesh as her tongue darted out to wet her lips.

That was all it took. One flash of that wet tongue combined with the ministrations of her hands and he was hard as a fucking rock. Unable to hide the tenting of his shorts, he shuffled slightly, changing the angle and hoping she wouldn't notice.

"There," she said, triumphant as she removed her hands and sat back on the grass. Lifting the bottle, she took a sip. "Feel better?"

Nodding, since he'd lost the ability to speak, he leaned forward and rested his arms over his knees, hoping like hell that would hide his massive boner. Feeling like a teenager who'd made it to first base, he was reminded how long it had been since a woman had touched him. Almost six years. Six long years of porn and his palm, in that same combination, over and over. The monotony was overwhelming.

Studying the woman across from him, Scott realized that he wanted to have sex with someone for the first time since he'd lost his wife. It was a strange thought since he'd been with Tina for so long. Their marriage hadn't been perfect but he'd loved her and desired her, never even contemplating being with other women as some of his other married buddies did. Scott believed in commitment and keeping that commitment to Tina had been easy.

When she passed, he struggled with the weight of the commitment, wondering if it meant he wouldn't ever feel comfortable being intimate with another woman. His therapist had informed him that was normal but eventually he would need to move on. That it wasn't fair to his wife or daughter to live a life where he couldn't experience happiness or fulfillment. At the time, it had sounded so strange. How did one move on when they'd lost so much?

But time had a way of easing pain if only in small increments and, eventually, the agony of the loss had devolved into a dull ache. Studying Ashlyn, he let the multitude of emotions swirl inside. Since the arousal was new, he felt the weight of it as it coursed through his body, wondering what the hell to do with it. After all, she'd mentioned an ex when they'd toured the home. Scott wondered whether it was an ex-lover, ex-boyfriend, or ex-husband. Regardless, even though he was feeling some pretty intense attraction toward her, she might not be interested, especially if the breakup was recent.

"Well, I guess I should let you get to work and I need to shower before I head into town again." She stood, wiping off her butt before extending her hand.

Gripping it, he let her pull him up, thankful the erection had abated, if only a little. "What's in town?"

"I'm going to meet with the mayor about adding my house to the haunted homes tour."

"Nice. Chad's a good guy."

"Excited to meet him."

They trailed around the building, returning to stand beside her car. "Well, thanks for the run. Hope we can do this a few times a week. And once you get used to running with me, I'd like to revisit starting a running club. It's going to get warmer soon and I promise it's fun."

"I didn't hate running with you," he said, smirking as he shrugged, "so maybe I'd be open to running with other people."

"We're evolving, Scott," she said, flashing a grin. "From annoying client to almost friendly neighbor who you don't hate spending time with. I like where this is going."

Laughing, he nodded. "Me too."

"Are you coming to Peter's cookout tomorrow? Carrie invited me."

"I'll be there. It's supposed to be a nice day."

"Great. Any pointers on what I should bring?"

Scott debated. "He doesn't drink so maybe a cake?"

"This coming from the man who hates chocolate?"

"How about a vanilla cake?"

Chuckling, she bit her lip as she considered. "I could do a yellow cake with cream cheese frosting. That sounds awesome. I'm in. Maybe you'll actually like this one."

"I liked the last one," he begrudgingly admitted.

"Mission accomplished." Lifting her fists in the air, she shook them. "Thanks for the water and the run. See you tomorrow."

Scott reached for the handle and pulled the door open. Closing it behind her, he gave a wave before she drove off. Hopping in his SUV, he grasped the handle above the window and clenched his fingers tight. Oh yeah, he was interested in his new client...neighbor...friend...or whatever she was becoming to him. Unsure what to do with the strange sentiment, he drove home to take a cold shower.

Chapter 11

Ashlyn completed a whirlwind of activities on Friday, including meeting with the mayor, baking the cake for the barbeque, and breaking down all the moving boxes so she could recycle them and create some space. When Saturday rolled around, she was eagerly anticipating the social gathering. Ashlyn had never met a stranger—a great quality to possess in her former profession—and she couldn't wait to meet more people in the small town she now called home.

Was she excited to see Scott? Hell yes. Ashlyn could still feel the prickly hairs of his legs against her palms, reminding her of the sweet torture she experienced yesterday while massaging his shin splints. The swirling desire caused her to question her celibacy pact as she searched her closet for something to wear. She'd made the pact because the thought of being intimate with anyone after Robert was overwhelming and a bit frightening. Although she hated it, his deception had made her question her self-worth. For someone as confident as Ashlyn, those feelings were certainly unwelcome.

"That bastard doesn't deserve to make you question anything," she mumbled to herself as she pulled the light sweater from the closet. Pairing it with jeans and flat boots, she finished her hair and makeup, grabbed the cake and bottle of prosecco, and headed to Peter's house.

Ten minutes later, she pulled up to a home situated on a large lot in a sprawling neighborhood. Armed with her offerings, she ambled around the tall wooden fence, approaching the sound of voices coming from the back.

"Hey, Ashlyn!" Carrie called, jogging over and opening the fence door. "Come on in. I'm so glad you found it."

"Thanks," she said, handing her the prosecco. "I figured bubbly and a homemade cake would do."

"Yum," she said, leading Ashlyn to a table covered by a bright plastic tablecloth. "Set it there, honey. Let me introduce you to Peter."

Once her hands were free, she placed one in the grasp of the man who now stood before her. "Peter Stratford," he said, shaking. "Boy, am I excited to meet you."

Ashlyn's eyebrows arched. "Is that so?"

"Oh, yeah." Excitement sparkled in his blue eyes. "You have no idea."

"Okay, I'm here to squash this conversation before it goes any further," Scott said, appearing at Peter's side. "Don't listen to a word he says. His favorite pastime is driving me insane."

"It's true," Peter said, shrugging before he patted Scott on the back. "This one needs some friendly jibing sometimes. Otherwise, I fall asleep when he's talking."

Scott glowered at him.

Lifting his hand to his mouth, he whispered loudly, "That means he's boring."

"All right," Carrie said, laughing as she grabbed Ashlyn's hand and led her toward the backyard. "Leave Scott alone. Come on, let me introduce you to my boys."

Two boys, the oldest with dirty-blond hair and the younger with a mop of brown hair, were kicking a soccer ball between them.

"Hey!" the younger one yelled when the oldest sent the ball whizzing past his head.

"Sebastian!" Carrie scolded. "No kicking above the waist. What did I tell you?'

"Sorry, Mom," he said, frowning. "He's just so slow."

"Am not!" the younger boy said, running toward Carrie and throwing his arms around her waist before burying his face in her shirt.

"Welcome to parenting," Carrie said, flashing a sardonic grin at Ashlyn. "It's magnificent."

Ashlyn chuckled as Sebastian asked, "Are you the woman with the ghost in your house?"

"Sure am," Ashlyn said, resting her palms above her knees and leaning toward him. "Her name was Sally Pickens and I'm pretty sure I heard her rocking in the chair in the attic earlier this week."

That spurred both boys to crane their necks and gape at her as their eyes grew wide. "No way," the younger one breathed.

"Yep. I'm Ashlyn," she said, extending her hand.

The boy buried his face back in Carrie's shirt before Sebastian walked over. "I'm Sebastian and that's Charlie," he said, shaking her hand. "I'm the oldest."

"It's nice to meet you, Sebastian. I'm an only child so I never had a younger brother. Is it fun?"

He shrugged. "It's okay. He's fun to play with sometimes."

"I like playing soccer," Charlie said, peeking up from Carrie's waist to make eye contact with her.

"Me too. I played on my high school team and we won the conference championship. Can I play with you guys?"

They both nodded excitedly before Charlie ran to grab the ball that rested beside the fence. They lined up across from each other and Sebastian gestured to her. "Come on. We can form a triangle and kick it to each other."

Carrie gave a sheepish grin. "You've done it now. They won't relent until you play with them."

"I'm game," Ashlyn said. "Maybe I can help them run off some energy and tire them out for bedtime."

"Well, you've just become my favorite person," she said, chuckling. "Have fun."

Ashlyn jogged over and jumped into position. "Okay, boys, let's see what you've got."

Scott sipped his soda as Peter droned in his ear about last night's basketball game. Although his friend didn't gamble on NBA games anymore, he still enjoyed watching. Scott nodded, agreeing with something Peter said although he had no idea what it was. Instead, his eyes were glued to Ashlyn as she played with Sebastian and Charlie. Shrills of laughter echoed through the yard and she was a natural, both with the kids and with her soccer skills. Having played basketball and soccer himself in school, he always appreciated a fellow athlete.

"And then I chopped off her head and moved to Mars," Peter said.

"That's great, man," Scott murmured.

Peter laughed. "Wow. You weren't even trying to listen. Pathetic."

Scott shot him a look. "You were talking about the Cavs, right?"

"Not even close," he said, taking a drink from his red plastic cup. "She's gorgeous."

"Yeah," Scott said, swallowing thickly.

"You've got to get back out there sometime, man."

Sighing, Scott rubbed the back of his neck. "Do I? I have no idea how to do that. Am I violating the commitment I made to Tina? I feel pretty torn up about it. And even if I got the courage to ask Ashlyn out, I'm nowhere near ready to offer something serious, which creates a conundrum since I have no clue how to be a casual dater."

"That's what happens when you marry your high school sweetheart. You never learn to love 'em and leave 'em. Thankfully, your ol' buddy here is an expert and ready to give you some advice."

"Can't wait to hear this," Scott said, rolling his eyes.

"Hey, don't knock it 'til you try it. Casual relationships can be fun, but you have to go into them with clear terms defined. I learned that the hard way, through lots of angry women and curse-filled text messages."

"Sounds fun. I'll pass."

Peter breathed a laugh. "Who knows what Ashlyn is open to? She came from the city, where people are a bit more laidback about dating and sex. Maybe she'd be willing to enter into a casual thing with you. You never know until you ask."

Scott gave him a droll glare. “So, what? I’m supposed to ask her on a date, mention I can only offer her casual sex with no strings attached, and hope she doesn’t punch me in the face? I don’t think I like the odds on that.”

“You’ll need a *little* more nuance than that,” he said, holding his thumb and index finger an inch apart. “But I learned after a while that women really dig honesty. Tell her exactly how you feel and what you want. Tell her that you haven’t been with anyone since Tina and what you’re able to offer. If she knows what you’re willing to give, she can debate and decide on whether to move forward or not. At least she’ll be going in with eyes wide open.”

“Maybe,” Scott said, sighing. “It’s a tough conversation to have when you’ve just met someone. I’m not sure she deserves to be saddled with my baggage.”

“Well, if she has an ex, she most likely has baggage too, and the beauty of casual relationships is that you don’t have to get too deep. Keep it light and fun. You can do it if you both are on board.”

Scott watched Ashlyn throw her arms in the air and cheer when Charlie made a particularly nice kick through the two-liter soda bottles they’d spaced apart as goals. He threw his arms around her and she laughed as she ruffled his hair. “I do have fun with her. It’s nice to hang out with a beautiful woman with a great sense of humor who loves Star Wars and running.” Kicking the grass with the toe of his sneaker, he said, “And with someone who doesn’t associate me with the accident.”

“I get it,” he said, cupping his shoulder. “What happened would be a huge burden for anyone, but here, where everyone knows your damn business, it’s that much worse.”

“I’m glad people remember Tina and Ella and I’m proud of the family we created. It’s just hard now that several years have passed. I think some people wonder why I haven’t moved on but I haven’t figured out what that looks like. Unfortunately, there’s no roadmap for these things.”

“People can suck it,” Peter said. “You move on in your own damn way on your own damn timeline. But you’re not a bad person if you take a step down a new path. If Tina had lost you would you have wanted her to remain alone forever?”

"No way."

"I know she felt the same. It's probably going to feel all sorts of strange but you're going to have to try again one day. Might as well be now."

Scott rubbed his hands over his face. "We're talking like she's already interested. Maybe she only sees me as her contractor and new jogging partner."

"Like I said, only one way to find out."

Mulling over the conversation, Scott finished his drink and set the cup on the table. "I'm itching to kick that ball while you fire up the grill."

"Go on," Peter said, glancing over to the patio where the grill sat. Carrie was deep in conversation with Chad Hanson, the mayor, and a few others. "I need to get crackin' anyway."

With a tilt of his head, Scott jogged across the yard. "Can I get in this game?"

Ashlyn flashed a beaming smile, causing his heart to lurch in his chest. "Only if you're ready to play. These two have skills." The boys both puffed their chests proudly.

"Ready. Let's see 'em."

Joining the revelry, Scott enjoyed the moment under the shining early-Spring sun.

Ashlyn had a fantastic time at the cookout, staying long past when the sun set behind the horizon. Finishing up her spiked seltzer, she realized it would be her last since she needed to get home and prepare for the week.

"I completed all the paperwork this morning," she said to Chad Hanson, the town's mayor who was drinking a beer alongside her. "I'll have it to your office Monday by noon."

"Fantastic," Chad said, saluting her with his beer. "It's always exciting to have another home on the haunted tour and Sally Pickens is legendary around here."

"Thanks for making it so easy, Chad. I'll need your help again when I apply for my food truck permits."

"We've never had a food truck in Ardor Creek," the mayor replied. "I love implementing new things around here and will be happy to help you."

"Thanks," she said, tossing her can and glancing at the table. "Well, looks like the cake was a hit. I'll go ahead and take the container home."

"Let me make a plate for you," Carrie said. "Give me a few." She buzzed around as Ashlyn said goodbye to everyone and returned with a huge tray of food. "Scott, why don't you carry this to Ashlyn's car so she can carry the Tupperware?"

"Oh, I can stack it—"

"It's fine," Scott said, taking the tray as Ashlyn gaped.

"That's enough leftovers for a week. I don't need that much, Carrie."

"The temperature is supposed to drop thirty degrees next week and we'll most likely get snow. Better to be stocked up."

Nodding, she hugged the kind woman. "Thank you," she whispered in her ear. "It was nice to be included."

"You're welcome, sweetie," she said, squeezing her.

"Ready?" Scott asked.

Grabbing the cake container, she followed him to the driveway and he stuffed the massive tray in her backseat. Smiling up at him, leaned against the car. "Looks like our runs might be canceled due to the weather next week."

He shrugged. "I can handle the cold if you can."

Her brows arched. "Is that a challenge?"

Chuckling, he nodded. "City folk don't have the constitution we have out here in the country."

"Oh, man, you've done it now. I can't wait to decimate you. Tuesday morning?"

"You're on." Reaching for the door, he opened it for her and she slid inside.

Once home, she unloaded the food—a menagerie of ribs, pasta salad, and other sides—thankful for Peter and Carrie's generosity. As she prepped for bed, she thought about the day and the wonderful people she'd met, cautiously optimistic that one day soon, she'd be seen as a local instead of the resident city girl.

Chapter 12

The next week brought bitter cold and snow, which allowed Scott to focus on the designs for Ashlyn's renovation. By Thursday, he was ready to file for permits but wanted to discuss them with her before he pulled the trigger. Picking up his cell, he phoned her, feeling his heartbeat accelerate as the rings shrilled in his ear.

"Calling to beg for mercy after I left you in the dust this morning?" her voice chimed.

"I'm pretty sure you were crying for your mama at one point, but I couldn't quite hear since I was so far ahead."

"*Pfft*," she replied, and he could almost see her eyes rolling through the phone. "You've got some revisionist history there, my friend."

"You did pretty well navigating around the snow. I'm impressed."

"We *do* have snow in New York City, Scott. Although it's mostly melted by now. Thank goodness because I prefer the heat to the cold any day."

"Me too. I'm hoping this was our last snow. Good news? It allowed me to hunker down and finish your designs. I was wondering if we could get together so I can go over them with you before I file for the permits tomorrow."

"Sure. Do you want to come over for dinner? I've finally slogged my way through Peter's leftovers and I was planning on cooking a meatloaf."

Scott's features scrunched. "I'm not a fan of meatloaf."

"Challenge accepted. Meatloaf it is."

A laugh escaped his throat. "I hate meatloaf more than chocolate."

"You're just solidifying my decision to make the best meatloaf ever. Keep going."

"Fine," he said, unable to control his smile. "I'll try it. Does six o'clock work?"

"Sure thing. See you then."

The phone clicked and he shook his head, amused at her persistence. A text appeared with a GIF of a woman shoving food in her face followed by a text that read: **This will be you tonight. Yum!**

The woman was funny. He'd give her that. Later, as he prepared to head to her house, Scott recalled his conversation with Peter as anticipation coursed through his veins. Would it be possible to initiate a conversation with Ashlyn about possibly taking their friendship to the next level? Would he be able to properly convey what he was willing to offer when he barely had any idea himself? Realizing the attempt to control a future conversation was futile, he shrugged on his coat and permitted himself to go with the flow. If the topic came up naturally, and she seemed interested in discussing it, he would dip his toe in the water.

After picking up some flowers and a bottle of red wine in town, he all but skipped up her front porch stairs, marveling at the excitement pulsing through his frame. When she opened the door, white teeth flashing from her brilliant smile, his knees almost buckled.

"Right on time," she said, extending her hands. "You've got a handful there. Let me help."

He handed her the wine and flowers, retaining the schematics as he followed her to the kitchen. She inspected the wine and set it on the island before smelling the flowers. "Wow, you sure know how to show up to dinner. These smell fantastic and I love cabernet."

"I'm glad," he said, shrugging off his coat. "Figured it never hurts to bring flowers."

"Let me grab a vase." Opening a cabinet above the sink, she stood on her toes as she pondered. "That one," she said, pointing. "Can you grab it for me?"

Trailing over, he reached for the vase, brushing against her as he grabbed it. Handing it to her, he was overcome by her scent as it surrounded him, so much more vibrant than the flowers. Feeling his muscles tense, he waited for her to take it.

"Oh, no, buddy. I'm putting you to work. Go ahead and fill it with water and place the flowers inside. You can set them on the dinner table. That's where we'll eat."

Maneuvering away, she bent over and checked the meatloaf, showcasing the firm globes of her ass in skin-tight jeans. Realizing he now was sporting a full-on erection, Scott filled the vase with water, thankful to have a task to take his mind off his pretty client.

They made easy conversation as she flitted around the kitchen. Once dinner was ready, she ushered him to the table and picked up the wine on the counter. "Should I open it?"

"I don't drink," he said from the round table that sat in the kitchen corner, "but you should have a glass."

After opening the wine and pouring a glass, she sauntered over and sat next to him. Waving a hand over the table, she showcased the feast she'd prepared. "Meatloaf, green beans, sweet potatoes, and butter rolls. Dig in."

They loaded their plates and Scott examined the meatloaf, noticing it appeared succulent and smelled fantastic. Spearing a bite with his fork, he dug in. Chewing the morsel, he was aware of Ashlyn's stare as his jaw worked. Lifting his gaze to hers, he swallowed before breaking into a grin. "Damn, it's really good."

"Success!" she cheered, throwing her hands in the air and giving a whoop. "I have no idea why this is so exciting but you made my damn week, Scott."

Chuckling, he ate another bite before murmuring, "Man, you are some cook, Ashlyn."

She seemed elated by the compliment and they fell into casual conversation as they ate. Ashlyn offered him homemade brownies for dessert but he leaned back in his chair and patted his stomach. "Sounds amazing but I'm about to burst. No wonder you run all the time. If I could cook like you, I'd need to burn a zillion calories every day."

"I love cooking," she said, standing and clearing their plates. Bringing over a cloth, she wiped the table. "Always have. There's something cathartic about it." Grabbing the plans, she brought them over and handed them to him. "Want to go over these here?"

Scott took the blueprints and spread them over the table, taking time to show her everything from the sweeping rebuilds to the intricate remodeling. Once finished, she bit her lip, excitement glowing in her deep green eyes. "These are amazing, Scott. Thank you. I'm so glad I stalked you until you took my job."

Breathing a laugh, he nodded. "I'm glad you stalked me too."

Her eyes roved over his face as she studied him, appearing as if she wanted to say more but hesitating. Finally, she asked, "Should we have a nightcap? I'd love one more glass of wine and I can make you coffee if you like."

"Coffee's perfect." He rolled up the schematics and took them to the car while she made the coffee and directed him to sit on the couch in the living room.

"Cream and sugar?"

"Black is fine," he said, relaxing back on the cushions. She returned with their drinks and sat on the couch, tucking her legs underneath as her dark hair seemed to glow in the light from the table lamp.

"Well, you survived meatloaf. I think I need a list of other things you don't like so I can make them and force you to reconsider."

"I'll get right on that," he said sardonically, taking a sip of coffee as she laughed. "Did you cook a lot in the city too?"

She looked to the ceiling as she contemplated. "I cooked when I could, although I worked a lot and rarely had time. I was the definition of a workaholic and it really burned me out after a while. But I enjoyed cooking nice meals on special occasions for me or my ex. You know, birthdays, holidays, and the like."

"Your ex made you cook your own birthday meals?"

"Better than him cooking. He was a terror in the kitchen. I'm not sure he knew how to boil water."

"Yikes," Scott said, curious to know more about her previous relationship. "How long were you together?"

"Four years. We got engaged about a year before we broke up."

His eyebrows lifted. “So, he’s an ex-fiancé?”

She tilted her head. “He’s an ex-fiancé.”

“I’m sorry it didn’t work out.”

She rolled her eyes. “Don’t be. He was an ass. I ignored so many signs. It was a really painful lesson and something I’m determined to never repeat.”

Scott contemplated her, desperate to pry but not wanting to overstep.

“I’ll just tell you,” she said, waving a hand. “It is what it is. The bastard cheated on me, maybe more than once, but the last time was verified. By me.”

“You saw them together?”

“Yep,” she said, running a hand through her hair. “I’d been in Colorado for a sales meeting and we wrapped up early. My flight home wasn’t until midnight but I was able to catch an earlier flight. Thought it would be romantic to come home early, cook dinner, and surprise him when he came home from work.”

“Oh, man,” he said, already anticipating where the story was going.

“Yeah, it sucks. I’m a stupid cliché. Traveling businesswoman who comes home early to find her partner in bed—*our* bed—with someone else. God, I was livid. I threw every blunt object I could find at his head but, sadly, he escaped without any concussions. Asshole.”

Compassion swamped him. “I’m so sorry, Ashlyn.”

Sighing, she gave a defeated shrug. “Shit happens. I’m determined to look at it as an opportunity to revamp my life. To start over and do things right this next cycle. I dodged a bullet with Robert but it definitely knocked me down a peg. I have no idea when I’ll be ready to enter into a relationship again. I told myself I’d remain single and celibate for a while to focus on me and rebuild.”

Scott ran his finger over the rim of his cup, pondering. “Celibacy can certainly help with that but it gets old after a while.”

Her eyes darted between his. “Have you been celibate since the accident?”

Expelling a deep breath, he nodded. “I have no idea how to be with someone else. Tina was my high school sweetheart.” He gave a sheepish grin. "She was my first and I thought she'd be my last. We broke up for a while in college and dated other people but once we got back together, that was it. I never even contemplated having to date or build another relationship. From what I hear, online dating is awful."

"My single girlfriends say it's terrible. Like, they'd rather bathe in acid."

Laughing, he shook his head. "Not an appealing endorsement. I just have no desire to do it. I'd rather remain alone. On the off chance something falls into my lap organically, I might consider it."

"Let me know when that happens. I'd love for Tom Hardy to show up at my door ready for an 'organic' relationship." Making quotation marks with her fingers, she snickered. "Can't wait."

"I hope it happens for you," he teased. "I'll be waiting for Emma Stone."

"Good choice," she said, pursing her lips. "Funny and pretty. You two will do well together."

Chuckling, he realized his cup was empty and Ashlyn had almost finished her glass of wine. "Well, I guess it's time I headed home. Thanks for dinner. It was great."

"You're welcome," she said, setting the glass on the table and standing.

He followed her to the door and shrugged on his jacket. "I know we weren't planning to jog tomorrow but I'm down if you are. We can fit in a run before I head to town and file for the permits."

"Sure," she said, smiling up at him. A wisp of her dark hair hung over her eye and before he could stop himself, he reached for it, gently tucking it behind her ear. A ragged breath escaped her lips at the soft touch. "Scott..." she whispered.

"Sorry," he said, drawing his hand back and dropping it to his side. Feeling like a coward, he reached for the door and pulled it open. "I didn't mean to...uh..." he struggled to finish the sentence.

"It's fine," was her gentle reply, as she held the door open. "Meet you in front of GDC at seven?"

Thankful to escape the uncomfortable situation, he nodded. "See you then." Giving her a salute, he trailed to his car, slamming the door behind him and gripping the wheel. The feelings swirling inside him were rampant and unnerving. Letting them fester, he tried to process them as he drove home.

Once in bed, he lay in the darkness, rubbing the pads of his fingers together, lost in the memory of Ashlyn's silky hair against his fingertips.

Chapter 13

By the end of the next week, Ashlyn was seriously reconsidering her celibacy pact. She thought she'd been firm in the decision but another week in close proximity with Scott had solidified what she'd already known deep inside: she wanted to bang her contractor. Hot, sweaty, steam-up-his-glasses, banging. By the time Friday rolled around, she'd imaged so many scenarios where she performed the horizontal tango with him, they were pretty much on a constant loop.

Although she was nowhere close to considering a serious relationship, she hated the fact that Robert had been her last lover. The more she thought about it, the more she wanted to erase any thought of sex with the scumbag from her memory. Cozying up to Scott would certainly accomplish that goal.

But what did Scott want? Ashlyn thought he was attracted to her but he was quite hard to read. Thinking back on their interactions, she recalled the times she'd sensed interest. After their meatloaf dinner, he'd tucked her hair behind her ear, those brown eyes seeming to smolder. She'd been so sure he was going to kiss her but he'd pulled away at the last moment, seeding her doubt. Was he interested or was she reading more into the situation?

Yesterday, after their jog, they'd sat in the meadow behind his office and he'd asked her to massage his shins again. Ashlyn had been taken aback at first but he'd just smiled sheepishly.

"You don't have to if you don't want," he'd said, his tone hesitant. "They're just killing me today."

"It's fine," she'd responded before sliding her hands over the hairy skin and maneuvering them over his flesh. Bouts of heat had flooded her body as arousal invaded her pores. When she finished, she wiped her damp palms on her shorts, the wetness a mixture from his exertion and her longing.

The phone rang on her kitchen counter, jolting her from the lascivious thoughts. Sliding the oven mitts from her hand, she held it to her ear. "Let me guess—you're calling to tell me you have the permit approvals?"

His deep chuckle reverberated through the phone. "Not yet but hopefully by the end of next week. Chad is working with the building commissioner to fast track them. I think he was smitten by you. If he wasn't hot and heavy with his current flame, I'd say you need to keep an eye out."

"I'm not above trading favors for permit approvals," she teased. "Everyone has their price."

"Noted. Who knew it was that easy?"

Laughing, she shook her head. "Only for some." For Scott? He could have a freebie. Or two. Or twenty. *Down girl.*

"So, what's up?"

"I have some new clients who recently moved from the city and they invited me over for dinner tomorrow to discuss their renovation schedule. One of the things I'm going to be building for them is a wine cellar. Apparently, he was a sommelier for some swanky restaurants in New York before he retired. I want to bring a nice bottle of wine for dinner but I don't have the first idea about what's good. The clerk at the liquor store helped me choose the bottle to bring to your house. My experience is limited to drinking Boone's Farm with Tina when we were teenagers."

Ashlyn wrinkled her nose. "Ew."

"Yeah, probably not the finest wine to take to a sommelier."

"No way. I could recommend some for you."

"You're reading my mind. I thought maybe you could meet me at the liquor store and help me look for something. I'd buy you a vodka soda or two at the pub afterward in return."

"You don't have to buy me anything for helping you scour the wine shelves. That's one of my favorite pastimes."

His sigh of relief filtered through the phone. "You're a lifesaver. I figured you'd probably know a ton about wine."

"I know enough," Ashlyn said, glancing at the ceiling as she contemplated. "Now I'm wracking my brain as to what to buy them. This is going to be fun. When should I meet you?"

"I'll be done at the office around three-thirty. Want to meet me at Wine and Spirits on Main Street at four? We can head to the pub afterward."

"Sure thing. See you then."

Clicking off the phone, Ashlyn blew a breath through puffed cheeks. If she didn't know better, she'd think Scott just asked her on a date. Sort of. Maybe. Okay, perhaps it was wishful thinking and he truly needed help selecting wine. Whatever it was, she headed to her bedroom to pick out an outfit that would knock his socks off.

Scott replaced the phone in the receiver on his desk and ran his hand through his hair. "God, I'm terrible at this."

"You did fine, man," Peter said, sucking on a peppermint as he sat on the other side of the desk. "She said 'yes' and now you can spend some time with her at the pub. Let the conversation happen naturally and see where it goes."

"I asked her to massage my shin splints the other day," he said, scowling. "I felt so stupid the second the words left my mouth but she'd done it once before and I thought it might be a good way to initiate something..." Trailing off, he shook his head. "This is really hard. How the hell do people date in real life? It's freaking awkward."

"Eh, it's okay once you get the hang of it," Peter said, shrugging. "From what I remember at least."

Scott studied his friend, struggling to understand why he still held himself back from Carrie. Although they'd had a terrible blow out years ago, she'd forgiven him and it was obvious to Scott she still carried intense affection for Peter.

"I feel like you're giving all the advice here, which I sorely need," Scott said, holding up a finger, "but I would be remiss if I didn't at least voice my opinion about you and Carrie."

The candy made a clacking sound between Peter's teeth as he scuttled it around his mouth with his tongue. "What opinion?"

"That you two should've never parted ways. I think you were always meant to be together."

Peter arched a sardonic eyebrow. "We were never you and Tina, Scott. We always had issues. First and foremost, her parents."

"It's hard dating the preacher's daughter," Scott said, his tone sympathetic. "No one would've been good enough for his little girl."

"Add in the fact that I moved to the city to make something of myself and turned into a degenerate, and I was screwed."

"But Carrie's parents aren't here anymore, and her shitbag husband is gone too. Good riddance."

Running a hand over his face, Peter sighed. "I should've never left that last time. I was afraid to settle down and get stuck here. Carrie was ready for it all—marriage, kids, the white picket fence, so I pushed her into that bastard's arms. I hate myself for it."

"Well, she managed to extricate herself from that disaster. She's pretty damn amazing."

"She is," he murmured, fingers twiddling in his lap. "But she's made it clear she only sees me as a friend. I ruined any chance I had with her." When Scott tried to say more, Peter held up a hand. "I don't want to discuss this, Scott. I'm sorry, but I need you to let it go."

Scott observed his friend's morose expression and took pity on him. "Okay, but I'm always here if you want to talk. In the meantime, we'll focus on my dating disasters. I'm sure I'll supply us with enough fodder for a thousand conversations."

Chuckling, Peter arched a brow. "Can't wait. Go get 'em, man."

A few hours later, Scott closed the tabs on his desktop and closed shop for the day, breezing past Carrie on the way out.

"Have fun at the pub!" she called to his back.

Whirling around, he gave her an incredulous stare. "I know this is a small town but there's no *way* you could've known I'm heading to meet Ashlyn."

"Peter told me," she said, shrugging as she gave him a knowing grin. "I think it's awesome, Scott."

"Don't tell anyone else," he said, holding up his index finger. "I mean it, Carrie."

"No way," she said, making an X over her heart. "I swear."

Giving her one last glower, he stalked to Wine and Spirits, feeling his heartbeat accelerate with every step. God, he was nervous. Stepping inside, he waved to Sean, the young clerk who worked afternoons and evenings at the store. Approaching the red wine section, he kept an ear open for the sound of the bell above the door. A few seconds later, he heard the *ding*, noting his heart was now beating at warp speed.

Turning, he observed a beaming Ashlyn walking toward him, her long, dark hair flowing behind her. She wore a silky sleeveless top, jeans, and some boot looking things with heels, giving her extra height. Feeling his Adam's apple bob, he lifted his hand and waved, realizing this would be the night everything would change. He didn't know *how*, exactly, but he'd never experienced attraction like this with anyone but Tina. Understanding how rare it was, Scott was ready to voice the sentiments to her. He didn't know what the hell he was going to say but figured it was best to be honest and straightforward. Excitement twined with the fear in his gut as she stopped only inches before him.

"Hi."

"Hi," he said, hating how gravelly his voice was. "Ready to help your wine-illiterate contractor?"

"Ready."

With that, they got to work.

Half an hour later, they sat at the bar in the pub, Ashlyn laughing at Scott's story about Peter's less than stellar basketball skills in middle school.

"How bad do you have to be to shoot in the other team's basket?" she asked in disbelief.

"Pretty bad. That was Peter's first and last basketball game. He figured out shortly thereafter that he was much better at poker and eventually ran the local high school card game for all the guys."

"No ladies?" Giving a *tsk, tsk, tsk*, Ashlyn shook her head. "I'm awesome Texas hold 'em. I would've decimated you guys."

"A card shark too?" he asked. "Is there anything you're *not* good at?"

Contemplating, she took a sip of her drink. "I'm not good at losing."

Laughing, he nodded. "As evidenced by your negotiating skills."

"Damn straight, buddy."

Glancing at his watch, Scott realized it was almost six o'clock. Dinnertime. Not wanting their time to end, especially since he'd decided this would be the night he told her about his...attraction? Feelings? Desire? Not knowing how to define it, he looked at her glass. "You're almost empty. If you'd like, we can go to my place and pop open the bottle you chose for yourself. There's a great Italian restaurant on Main Street that has quick delivery."

Those deep green eyes searched his face before she downed the rest of her drink. "I think we should go to my place. I left bread rising in the oven and need to take it out. Also, I feel like there are some things we need to say to each other and I want home-field advantage."

The corner of his lips curved. "I love what a straight shooter you are, Ashlyn."

Her brows lifted. "Good, because I think we've been dancing around some things and I'm not going to hold back. Are you ready for this discussion?"

Inhaling a deep breath, he nodded. "I'm ready."

"Good. Let me get the check and we'll blow this joint." She lifted her hand to signal to the bartender.

"I can get it—"

"No way," she said, taking the check the man handed her and placing her credit card on top before sliding it back. "You bought me an awesome bottle of wine, which you totally didn't have to do, and you only drank iced tea for goodness sakes."

Once the bill was closed, they headed to their cars and back to Ashlyn's home. She told Scott to make himself comfortable and made coffee before flitting around the kitchen. He sat on the island stool as they chatted. She was a whirlwind, removing the bread from the oven before whipping up a stir-fry for dinner.

"I swear, this wasn't a backhanded attempt to get you to cook for me again," he said, ingesting another bite of the delicious stir-fry as they sat at the kitchen table.

"I know but isn't it good?" Her eyes sparkled as she chewed.

"Heaven," was his sated reply.

Once finished, she poured herself a glass of the wine he'd bought her earlier and he refilled his coffee. "So," she said, gesturing to the front door, "I think it's best if we talk on the porch. Lots of fresh air so our thoughts can ruminate."

"I like it," he said, following behind her as she trailed outside. The weather was warmer this week but still chilly and he asked if she wanted her coat.

"The wine will keep me warm," she said, lifting her glass. Leaning against the wooden railing, he stood beside her, a few feet separating them. Setting his cup on the rail, he placed his hands flat, searching for the right words.

"I don't want this to be awkward," she said, "but it's probably best if you at least face me while we talk."

Grinning, he turned to lean his hip against the wood. "Sorry. I really want to say the right thing here, Ashlyn, and I have no idea what it is."

Her expression was so open, those pretty lips curved in such a genuine smile, that he relaxed immediately. "Neither do I, so at least we're on the same level."

His lungs felt constricted as he processed his words. "I'd convinced myself that I was fine. That life was good and I was content. I never even imagined being with anyone else after Tina."

"Why would you? She was your wife. You took vows, Scott. I've never met anyone who made it to that point with me. Believe me, when I speak words that important, they'll mean something."

"They definitely meant something," he said with a nod. "And one of the most important things we pledged was 'til death do us part. I never contemplated having to examine that phrase until we were both old and gray."

Compassion swam in her eyes, causing something to swell in his chest. "I'm so sorry," she whispered.

"I know," he said, closing his eyes to gather his thoughts. "Everyone's always sorry." Lifting his lids, he shrugged. "What's so awesome about you is that the sorrow doesn't cloud every interaction we have."

"Nope." She bit her lip. "I'm just a newbie here."

A laugh escaped his throat. "You're doing pretty well so far. Everyone in town is smitten with you."

"Everyone?" she asked, her voice raspy.

Stepping forward, he closed the distance between them. Taking her glass, he set it beside his cup on the rail. Gliding his hands over the soft skin of her neck, he gently tilted her head. Feeling as if his heart might pound out of his chest, he stared deep into those limitless eyes. "Everyone, Ashlyn. Even your grumpy contractor." She giggled as he grinned. "I sure as hell wasn't ready for you, but you're here and if there's anything I've learned, it's not to waste a single day on an opportunity to seize happiness."

Her resulting smile was gorgeous. "Am I an opportunity to you, Scott?"

"Yes," he almost whispered. "An opportunity to feel so many things I told myself I'd never feel again. Friendship. Affection. Desire."

Her throat bobbed. "You have friends."

"None like you."

"Surely you've been attracted to someone else over the past few years."

"Not one fucking person." His fingers slid into the hair at the back of her neck, gently squeezing. "No one 'til you. It scares the hell out of me."

His body pulsed, gently bushing hers as her chest lifted with rapid breaths. “I took a celibacy pact.”

Smiling, he lowered his head, nuzzling her nose with his. “I won’t tell anyone if you don’t.”

The timbre of her laugh surrounded him in warmth as she slid her hands up his chest and latched them behind his neck. “Are you ready for this, Scott? We’re both still coming to terms with our pasts.”

Lowering his lips, he gently brushed them against hers, loving her resulting hiss. “No fucking way. But I’m going to kiss you anyway.”

Latched onto his gaze, she sucked his bottom lip between hers, pulling on the tender flesh. Unable to process anything but her touch, Scott fisted his hand in her hair and enveloped her mouth with his.

Chapter 14

Ashlyn had no idea what sound escaped her mouth when Scott devoured her lips, but it was laced with all the pent up desire she'd been holding inside. Clutching him tight, she lifted to her toes, her tongue thrusting against his as they tasted each other for the first time.

Groaning, Scott slid his hand down to rest on her lower back, drawing her so close she thought they might fuse together. As his tongue slid over hers, wet and silky, he jutted his erection against her, the firm length proof that his desire mimicked hers. Needing more, she lifted her leg, twining it around his thigh, pulling him into her body.

With a desire-laden growl, Scott lowered his hands to her ass, squeezing the firm globes through her jeans before lifting her. Giving a yelp, she held on for dear life as he sat her atop the porch railing. As he drew her close, she locked her ankles behind his back and thrust her fingers into his thick brown hair.

"I've got you," he whispered before claiming her lips again, devouring the swollen flesh as he undulated his body against hers. They moved in the oldest rhythm of time, clutching each other as they tasted...and nibbled...and teased...

Breaking the kiss, he rested his forehead on hers, panting as if they'd just finished one of their runs. Fisting her hair in his hand, he stared into her eyes. Ashlyn felt the intensity of his gaze, eliciting a shaft of fear in her heart.

"You okay?" he asked softly, nuzzling her nose.

"Yes," she whispered, nodding. "It's just pretty intense. I haven't felt this much passion for someone in a long time."

Brown irises darted between hers, filled with curiosity.

Shrugging, she said, "Robert and I weren't really intimate in the last year of our relationship. We lost the spark. I wondered if it was me." Tightening her legs, she squeezed him. "But I definitely feel a spark with you."

"I don't really want to think about you with your ex, but let me just say, he's an absolute idiot. Any man who would betray you isn't worth the dirt on the bottom of your cute little shoes."

Chuckling, she asked, "You like them? I was trying to knock your socks off, hoping this might happen."

"I like them," he all but growled. "I like so many things about you, Ashlyn."

Stroking his hair, she expelled a breath. "I like you too, you know. When I first saw you with your shirt off, I knew I was in trouble."

Laughing, he stole a sweet kiss from her lips. "I might have been too pissed to recognize it then but by the time we started jogging together, I couldn't deny my attraction to you."

One of her eyes squinted shut. "Were your shin splints *really* hurting the other day?"

"Nope," he said, flashing a brilliant smile. "I was searching for an excuse for you to touch me. I'm really terrible at flirting, by the way."

"You're not so bad." She gave him a wink before straightening atop the railing. "Okay, I love this whole lift me against your body and ravish me thing, but I do think it's important we set some ground rules here. We've both got a lot of history and I'm determined not to make the same mistakes I made before."

Nodding, he gripped her butt before lifting her and setting her on her feet. Gesturing to the two rocking chairs, she said, "Let's sit."

Scott lowered into the chair and she did the same, staring at the darkened horizon as she gathered her thoughts. "I think it's important to be honest with each other." Reaching over, she squeezed his wrist as it sat atop the armrest. "I don't want to ask you for anything you're not ready to give."

Scott's lips pursed as he contemplated. Inhaling a breath, he said, "I have no idea what I'm capable of giving. That's my honest assessment here. You're the first person I've even contemplated being with since Tina. I'm so attracted to you and want to make love to you, but I'm not sure what I can offer beyond the physical aspect." Taking her hand, he laced their fingers. "I'm sorry if that's shitty but I don't want to make you false promises."

"I've had enough false promises," she said, squeezing his hand. "Brutal honesty will get you everywhere, my friend." Leaning her head back against the chair, she deliberated. "I think I'd be okay just starting with a physical relationship. Although I took a celibacy pact, it might do wonders for me to have some hot, sexy times to remind myself I've still got it."

"You've definitely got it," he murmured, arching a brow.

Laughing, she tilted her head. "Thank you. That bastard knocked me down a few pegs and I think it's healthy to get back out there. But what about the other things? Dating? Exclusivity? Where do you stand on that stuff?"

Scott blinked as he pondered. "I don't think it's fair to ask you to be exclusive if I'm not ready to offer you something in return. I wish I was there, Ashlyn, but I'm just not. But, to be frank, I have no desire to be with anyone but you."

"Neither do I," she said, clenching her hand in his. "So, what would make you comfortable? Perhaps we need to lay some ground rules. No sleeping over or expectations of a commitment for now. Two adults having a fun affair to get back on the horse, so to speak."

"I think I can do that," he said, eyes narrowed. "And I think it's time for me to take that step. I'm fine with not sleeping over yet because that's one step from co-habitation, which I'm not ready for, but I still want to hang out with you. Obviously, we have our runs, and we can still go to the pub and other places together. I really enjoy spending time with you."

"I like spending time with you too, Scott. So much."

He tugged on her hand and she stood. Approaching his chair, she placed one knee beside his hip before the other. Straddling him, she shimmied over his crotch before sliding her arms around his neck. "I think we're pretty much on the same page, then," she said, softly brushing her lips against his.

"The last thing to air out is the fact I'm your contractor," he said, gliding his hands to cup the mounds of her butt. Heat seeped through the denim, causing wetness to gush at her core. God, his hands were huge. She couldn't wait to have them on every inch of her body.

"Are you afraid we're crossing some sort of ethical line?"

"I don't think we are as long as we acknowledge there are risks. If this goes badly, you could sue me in retaliation or something along those lines."

"Or, you could surreptitiously do faulty work to get back at me if this ends in disaster," she teased.

"I'd never do that," he said, features drawn together.

"I know, and I'd never sue you for retaliation or whatever else you can think of. We're adults here, Scott. Things don't work out sometimes and that's life. I promise not to take it out on you if this somehow goes down the drain, although I don't see that happening."

"I promise to do pristine work even if you end up driving me crazy."

"Hey," she said, pouting.

Chuckling, he slid his fingers into her hair, drawing her close. "I'm kidding. You already drive me crazy and I'm still mad for you, so we're good."

Rubbing her lips over his, she bit the flesh. "You love that I drive you crazy. I think you needed someone to throw you off balance."

"And you need someone to remind you how gorgeous and amazing you are," he whispered, enveloping her lips in a sweet kiss. "Let me show you how magnificent you are."

"Show me," she murmured, hugging him tightly. "Carry me upstairs and fucking show me."

Heeding her command, her sexy-as-hell contractor lifted from the chair, clasping her body to his, and transported them inside.

Once they were beside her bed, Scott lowered her, setting her feet on the floor. Gazing over her flushed cheeks, he suddenly felt nervous.

"We'll take it slow," she said softly, gliding her palms over his dress shirt. Clasping the top button, she freed it before moving to the next one…and the next one. Tugging the shirt, she freed it and finished unlatching the buttons. Spreading it wide, she sucked in a breath. "There's that sexy chest." Rubbing her hands over the scratchy hairs, she smiled. "How in the hell does a contractor who's in the office most of the time have such a fantastic body?"

"I think it's the running. It's something I really enjoy. Even more, now that I have such a pretty jogging partner."

Biting her lip, she continued caressing his skin. "There's no expectation here, Scott. Anything we do together will feel good."

"I guess you can tell I'm nervous as hell," he said, cupping her shoulders and sliding his hands over her silky blouse. "It's been a long time for me."

"I've got you," she said, repeating his earlier words.

"We've got each other," he whispered.

Nodding, she grasped the back of his neck, tugging him toward her.

Joining his lips to hers, he kissed her as they shrugged away their clothes—first their shirts, then their shoes, pants, and underwear until they were bared to each other. Urging her toward the bed as his tongue tangled with hers, she fell onto the brown comforter, laughing as he crawled over her.

"Crap, you're laughing," he said, grinning.

"It's a good laugh," she said, opening her legs so he could settle between them. "I feel so free right now. God, I love it."

Taken by her glowing skin, he plunged his tongue back into her mouth before trailing kisses down her neck and over her collarbone. When he reached her breast, he nuzzled the pert nipple with his nose. "What do you like?" he asked, staring into her gorgeous eyes.

"Slow licks before you suck them."

"Mmm..." Extending his tongue, he ran it over the pebbled bud, feeling like a conquering gladiator when her back arched upon the bed.

"Yes," she purred, thrusting her nails into his scalp and upper back as she clutched him. "Oh, god."

Spurred on by her sexy little mewls, he continued to lather her nipple, licking and teasing it with the tip of his tongue before sucking it between his lips. Encouraged by reaction and the flush of red upon her skin, he played with her until the nipple was taut and kissed his way to the other little nub. Repeating the same ministrations, he watched her squirm, his dick so hard as it pressed against the soft skin of her thigh, he prayed he wouldn't blow it like a teenager. Blood pounded through his frame as she writhed below him, and Scott reveled in how beautiful she was as she experienced the pleasure.

Wanting to taste her, he placed a chaste kiss on each of her now-turgid nipples before kissing a path down her abdomen. Delving his tongue into her navel, she giggled below him.

"Ticklish," she moaned.

"Sorry," he murmured, giving her a sly smile.

"No, you're not." She bit her lip as she clutched his hair. "Keep going. I'm definitely not ticklish the lower you go."

Chuckling, his lips trailed over the small strip of hair above her mound before kissing the juncture of her folds. Palming her inner thighs, he pushed them apart to find her glistening in the soft light of the bedside lamp.

"Fuck," he whispered, sliding his index finger through the wetness. "You're dripping, honey."

"I'm so into you, Scott," she said, shrugging against the mattress. "I'm like this a lot around you."

"Even when we're jogging?" he asked, brows arching.

Biting her finger, she gave a seductive nod.

"Holy shit," he breathed, gazing at her swollen, wet pussy. "You know that's all I'm going to think about when we run now, right?"

That induced another nod, her hair splaying behind her like a magnificent Greek goddess as she gazed at him, sultry and sly.

Pressing his finger against her opening, he gently began to push inside.

"Oh, yes," she cried, lids cementing shut as she threw her head back. "More, Scott. Please."

Desperate to please her, he inserted another finger, sliding it along the tight, wet channel. The muscles of her core clenched him, causing him to grit his teeth in anticipation of sliding his cock into the taut vise. Unable to hold back any longer, he pulled out of her and spread her folds apart with both hands before burying his face in her honeyed center.

Thin fingers threatened to pull the hair from his head as she drew him close. Scott worked his tongue, jutting it inside her deepest place before sliding it up to lick the tight bud that was now exposed.

"Flick it just like that," she cried in a voice he'd never heard her use. "If you keep doing that I'll come."

Determined to make that happen, he kept up the ministrations as her body tensed and trembled beneath. Suddenly, she snapped, her nails squishing so far into his skull, he'd tease her for it later. Screaming his name, she clenched her thighs against him and gave in to the orgasm.

Scott gently sucked the pulsing flesh as she floated, loving the sweet taste that was Ashlyn. Eventually, she fell back to Earth, sighing in contentment as her grip released, if only a little.

"For the love of all that's holy," she groaned, replete upon the comforter. "You damn near took me to heaven, Scott."

Chuckling, he nuzzled the still quaking, wet flesh. "You taste so good, sweetheart, and you're so gorgeous when you come. Even if I end up with a slight concussion."

Contrition entered her gaze as she stared down at him. "Crap. Did I puncture you? I'm a beast with my nails. I'm so sorry."

Leaning his cheek on her inner thigh, he smiled as she stroked his hair. "It's all worth it to see you look at me like you are now, all sexy and sated. You're so fucking beautiful, Ashlyn."

He thought he saw the glimmer of tears in her eyes before she gently tugged his tresses. "Get up here and bang me now. Unless you want me to suck you in return?" She waggled her brows. "I'll be happy to."

Grinning, he extricated from her and stood. Leaning down, he pulled his wallet from his pants and pulled out the condom. "I definitely want that, but let's wait until next time."

"Yes, sir," she said, giving a good-natured salute as her body lay limp upon the bed. "Thank god, because I'm depleted."

After he rolled the condom on, he slid back over her, finding the spot between her thighs where his body fit so perfectly. "I'm glad it felt good."

"It felt so good," she said, palming his cheeks. "Now it's your turn."

Finding her opening with the tip of his shaft, he gripped the base to help himself begin to ease inside.

"You won't hurt me," she said, her eyes so deep as she stared up at him. "Go as hard as you want. I like it that way."

Feeling something inside him roar, he began to jut inside, inch by inch, feeling her swallow him whole with each new thrust.

"You're so tight, Ashlyn. *Fuck*."

"You feel so good," she whimpered, head shaking on the bed. "*Harder*."

Armed with her consent, he began to undulate into her, his hips moving in long, sure thrusts as she moaned below him. Overcome with the gravity of being intimate after so many long, lonely years, Scott felt something inside shatter before attempting to piece back together.

"I'm here," Ashlyn whispered, staring into his soul as she sensed the sentiments whirling inside him. "I've got you."

"*Ashlyn...*"

"I know, sweetheart," she said, her expression so open and understanding.

Feeling so connected to her, in ways he'd never expected, he rested on his forearms before sliding his fingers into her hair. Hammering inside her, his eyes locked with hers, unable to look away. They rode each other, raw and exposed until her tight channel threatened to choke him.

"I'm going to come," he said through gritted teeth.

"Yes," she cried, lifting her hips to meet his frenzied thrusts.

"Are you...?"

"It feels amazing," she said, placing her fingers over his lips. "Keep going."

Cementing his lips to hers, he enveloped her in a sweeping kiss as he hammered into her desire-ravaged body. Feeling his balls tighten, he clenched his fingers in her silky hair. She moaned his name, the sexy timbre of her voice causing him to lose all control. Feeling his muscles snap, he gave in to the pleasure and let go.

Warm, pulsing jets shot into the condom as he clutched her tight, burying his face in her neck as she held on for dear life. Bucking into her snug warmth, he saw stars as he emptied himself inside her pulsing body. Thin arms encircled his back, drawing him against her wet skin. Lost in her taste and smell, Scott felt the joy of sated sexual contentment for the first time in so long.

Unable to move, he languished in the moment, reveling in the feel of her nails as they tenderly scraped across his shoulder blades. Wishing he never had to move again, he placed sweet, sloppy kisses along her sweat-soaked neck.

"Man, I was rusty at that. I'm not sure how long I lasted but I'm pretty sure you didn't come while I was inside you. I'm sorry."

Her finger tapped on his back, causing him to lift his head. Ashlyn beamed back, looking like a sated seductress. "Um, hi. Do you see me complaining?"

Grinning, he shook his head. "Nope. You look pretty content."

Sighing, her head relaxed further into the pillow. "So fucking content. That was awesome."

"Thank goodness." Placing a peck on her lips, he began to slide out, already missing her wrapped around his sensitive length. "Let me get rid of the condom. Be right back."

Once he'd taken care of business in the adjoining bathroom, he sauntered back to find her resting under the covers, her dark hair splayed over the pillow. "I know we're not doing sleepovers but you can hold me for a little while before you bail. If you want." She gave a hesitant smile.

Lifting the covers, he slid beside her and drew her back into his front. "I definitely want," he said, kissing the rim of her ear.

"Mmm...that feels good." Shimming her ass into his crotch, she yawned. "I usually pass out after sex. Feel free to leave whenever and lock the bottom lock behind you. I won't be mad. Promise."

"Okay," he said, stroking the smooth skin of her upper arm. It had been so long since he held someone like this and it was...strange. Nice and new, yet old and familiar, all at once. "Ashlyn?"

"Hmm...?"

"Thank you for..." struggling to find the words, his brow furrowed.

"You're welcome," she said softly. "I know this was a big step for you, Scott."

"It was," he said against her shoulder. "I'm so glad it was with you."

"Me too," she whispered.

Snuggling into him, her body slowly relaxed until her breathing grew slow and heavy. Grateful for her understanding demeanor, he held her until his eyes begin to droop. Hating to leave her, he gently disengaged from her body. Once dressed, he stared down, stroking the hair at her temple but careful not to wake her.

After several reflective moments, Scott headed down the stairs, locking the door behind him before driving home. Once he'd brushed his teeth and prepped for bed, he laid in the darkness, contemplating the choice he'd made. The image of Tina's smiling face wafted through his mind and he felt a sense of peace. Rubbing his hand over his heart, he realized she would've loved Ashlyn, with her fiery wit and go-getter mentality. And there, in the shadowed room, he reconciled his decision to move on. Tina would want him to be happy, and Ashlyn spurred more happiness inside his broken heart than anyone had in so very long.

Vowing not to throw that happiness away, Scott closed his eyes and fell to sleep.

Chapter 15

Ashlyn woke the next morning and stretched, yawning as her spent muscles decompressed. Feeling her lips curve, she noted her soreness down below. Scott had a pretty nice package to go along with that delicious chest. Excited to see the goods again, she picked up her phone, wondering what to do now. Should she text him? Maybe something light and funny? Gnawing her lip, she contemplated.

The ground rules they'd set made sense since neither one of them were ready for a relationship. She was still getting over Robert's betrayal and Scott was slowly opening himself to a sexual encounter with someone besides his wife. Man, they were two peas in a pod with all their combined issues, although Scott's was a stroke of terrible luck whereas hers was a product of misunderstandings and mistakes.

"Well, Robert's in the past for good now, Ashlyn," she murmured to herself. "Good freaking riddance." Giving a little squeal, she rose, deciding she'd give Scott time to text her before she reached out to him.

An hour later her phone dinged and she lit up as bright as the screen when she read Scott's text.

Scott: Well, I think this is long enough to wait to text you, right? I have no idea how to do this. Take pity on me and remember I was in my twenties when I last tried to seduce someone.

Laughing, her thumbs composed a text back.

Ashlyn: You're doing a pretty good job. Not stalkerish at all. How old are you anyway? I'm thirty-three and figure you're around fifty since I leave you in my dust every time we jog.

Scott responded with an eye roll emoji before the text bubble appeared.

Scott: I'm thirty-eight and will immediately stop slowing down on the curves like I always do when I wait for you.

Ashlyn: In your dreams, grandpa. Anyway, how are you today?

She wanted to ask more but felt that texting was so impersonal. He'd taken a huge step last night after several years of celibacy and she didn't want to make him uncomfortable.

Scott: I'm good. Great actually. I think I dreamed of you. Weird, since I usually don't dream anymore.

Aw. Taken by the sweet comment, she searched for something poignant to write back.

Ashlyn: I really liked falling asleep in your arms. That's probably super sappy so just tell me to shut up if it's too much. But I had a nice time with you. Thank you, Scott.

Scott: Nice enough to hang again tonight?

Ashlyn's eyebrows narrowed as she remembered he had his client dinner tonight.

Scott: The Robinsons said I could bring a guest but don't feel obligated. If you want to join me, I'd love to have you. Completely up to you.

Feeling her heart slam into overdrive, she couldn't say yes fast enough.

Ashlyn: Of course, I'd like to come. Thank you so much for asking me.

Scott: Whew. Okay, great. I get really nervous every time I ask you something like that. I'll pick you up at six-thirty. Sound good?

Ashlyn: It's so cute you get nervous but here's a pro tip: I'll always say yes to you. And, yes, six-thirty is fine. I'll be ready.

Scott: See you then.

She shot him a smiley face before deciding to work in the garden. Now that they'd hopefully had their last snow, she was ready to begin planting. Feeling her body buzz in anticipation of seeing Scott, she gathered her gardening equipment and got to work.

Ashlyn watched Scott pull up at six-thirty on the dot and trailed down the porch stairs. Before she could hop in the passenger side, he jogged over and opened the door for her.

"I think you're the last man on Earth who still does that," she said, beaming up at him.

"I might have an ulterior motive," he said, inching closer.

"Ohhh..." Sliding her arms around his neck, she aligned her front with his. "Does this ulterior motive involve kissing me?"

"Fuck yes," he whispered, sprawling his hand across her lower back before drawing her closer. "Come here."

This kiss was urgent, his lips pressing hers open so he could sweep her mouth with his tongue. Tiny sparks of pleasure burned in every cell of her skin as she clutched onto him. Twining her tongue with his, she licked and sucked, showing him how much she'd missed him, although it had only been hours.

"Wow," he murmured, resting his forehead against hers. "I wondered if I'd only imagined how good you taste."

"And?"

"Like heaven, honey," he said, placing one last sweet kiss on her lips. The endearment made all sorts of feelings swirl inside her stomach and she told herself to get a grip. This thing with Scott was sexual and it was natural to whisper cute names while experiencing passion. It didn't represent more and she certainly wouldn't delude herself it did. Delusions had led her down the disastrous path with Robert and she would *not* make those mistakes again.

"You okay?" Scott asked, concern in his eyes.

"I'm good," she said, waving her hand. "Starving, too. Wonder what Mrs. Robinson is cooking for dinner?"

"No idea," he said, closing the door once she was seated inside. Sliding into the seat, he started the car and used one of his broad hands to turn the wheel. When had turning a steering wheel become sexy? Ashlyn had no idea but she could watch him drive all damn day.

"Ashlyn?"

"Sorry, what?"

"I said, no matter what she prepares, it won't be anywhere near as delicious as your cooking. But I'm sure it will still be good."

"Thank you," she said, elated he enjoyed her cooking. They made easy conversation until they arrived at the home. It was in a lovely neighborhood and she was excited to meet new people.

Scott parked in the driveway and they headed up the stairs, the fancy bottle of wine she'd picked out in his hand. He knocked and a salt-and-peppered-haired man answered the door, a huge smile on his face.

"Hello, Scott," he said, extending his hand for a shake. "Lynn and I are so tickled to have you over. You're our first guests in the new house." Extending his hand to Ashlyn, he said, "William Robinson."

"Hello, Mr. Robinson," she said, shaking his hand. "Ashlyn Rivers. So nice to meet you."

"Will is just fine, dear, and the pleasure is mine. Come on in."

They entered the foyer, hanging their light jackets before Scott extended the wine. "I can't take credit for this. Ashlyn picked it out. She's the wine expert in this twosome."

"Expert is a bit of a stretch," she said, grinning, "but I do love a good red."

"Bouchaine is an excellent brand," Will said, impressed. "Not very well known, though."

"I discovered them on a trip to Napa several years ago and love everything they produce."

Looking at Scott, Will said, "Keep this one, my boy. A good woman who knows about good wine is hard to find."

Chuckling, Scott gave a nod. "Will do. Can we help you or Lynn with anything?"

"Oh, no, you two come on in and we'll have a glass of rosé while Lynn finishes the meatloaf."

Ashlyn almost burst out laughing as Scott's eyes grew wider. "Meatloaf," he repeated.

"Yes. My wife is a fantastic cook. You both like meatloaf, right?"

"Oh, I like it but Scott *really* loves it. In fact, it's his favorite."

Scott shot her a murderous glare as she desperately tried not to devolve into hysterical laughter right there in the foyer.

"Well, how fortuitous," Will said, leading them into the living room. "Have a seat there on the couch and I'll be right back with the rosé."

"I don't drink but I'd love a water," Scott said.

"Sure thing. Ashlyn?"

"Oh, rosé all day for me. Bring it on."

With a twinkle in his eye, he disappeared around the corner. Lowering onto the couch, Ashlyn snickered as Scott glowered at her. "You're going to pay for this," he muttered.

"Oh, come on," she said, shrugging. "It's probably not that bad. You liked my meatloaf."

"You're the best cook I've ever met. We'll see. I'll do my best to stomach it."

Basking in his praise, she took the champagne glass from Will when he returned and they had a lovely conversation before Lynn eventually made an appearance.

"Hello, Scott," she said, shaking his hand as he stood. "Oh, no, please stay there. Only a few more minutes and dinner will be ready." Glancing at Ashlyn, she said, "It's so lovely to meet you. I hear you're from Manhattan."

"I lived there for most of my adult life but now I've relocated here. It's different but...nice. So far, I love it."

"Well, we're happy to know another New Yorker. Will was hesitant to leave the city once we both retired but I needed a change of pace."

"I can understand that."

"Bring them into the dining room in five minutes, dear," Lynn said to Will before heading back to the kitchen.

Once they were seated at the large table, Will gave a toast to meeting new friends and Ashlyn took a sip of the fabulous Bouchaine pinot noir. Letting it roll over her tongue, she closed her eyes at the full texture and slight tartness.

"It's fantastic, Ashlyn," Will said, lifting his glass. "Thank you."

"Well, Scott bought it. I just helped pick it out."

"I appreciated the assist," Scott said, winking at her before lifting the first bite of meatloaf to his lips. She noticed the hesitancy and the flaring of his nostrils as he began to chew. It was obvious he hated it. Pursing her lips, she vowed not to laugh as she began to enjoy the meal. It wasn't bad by any stretch, but her meatloaf was much better, in her humble opinion.

They spent most of the dinner discussing the renovations before the conversation turned to Will's former job as a sommelier and Lynn's thirty-year teaching career. Ashlyn found the couple lovely and was happy to connect with other "city slickers", as Scott called them in his teasing way as Lynn served desert.

"I still can't believe you were the sommelier for DeNovo in Midtown," Ashlyn said to Will as she finished her cheesecake. "I've taken a hundred doctors to dinner there to discuss new products. We've definitely crossed paths."

"I really enjoyed it," he said, taking a sip of the dessert wine he'd poured after dinner. "And what will you do now that you've left the corporate world, Ashlyn?"

"I'm going to start my own food truck, with organic offerings I can serve around town. I have no idea how to even begin and will probably fall flat on my ass at first, but if there's one thing I've learned, you have to pick yourself up and keep going until you get it."

"What an amazing young lady you are," Lynn said, smiling at Scott. "You need to hold on to this one, dear."

"She's pretty remarkable," Scott said, grinning down at her. The sentiment in his eyes was so poignant, she damn near forgot to breathe.

"I don't want to bring up anything that will sour the mood," Lynn said, "but we heard what happened to your wife and daughter all those years ago, Scott. I can't imagine how difficult that was. Will and I lost our son in Iraq many years ago and it was devastating."

"I'm so sorry to hear that," Scott said, giving them a sympathetic smile. "Losses like that are debilitating, as I'm sure you understand. It was hard to move on without feeling guilt or really intense sorrow. Ella had just started talking and Tina was the love of my life, so it was overwhelming for many years. Now, it's become a dull ache and I try my best to move forward knowing that's why they would've wanted."

Ashlyn sat beside Scott, the spoken words between the dinner guests reduced to unintelligible gibberish as she struggled to process his words. *Tina was the love of my life.* Of course, she was. It made so much sense in Ashlyn's logical brain. Scott had been married and he'd loved his wife to distraction. Why wouldn't he? No matter what woman entered his life, she would only have the opportunity to be with Scott because circumstances had denied him from being with the one he truly wanted.

Feeling a burning sensation in her chest, Ashlyn absently rubbed her heart, not even realizing she was performing the gesture until Scott's muffled voice sounded in her ear.

"Ashlyn?"

Blinking slowly, she turned her head, wondering why everything was now happening in slow motion.

"Ashlyn?" Scott repeated, worry crossing his handsome features. "You okay?"

"Yeah," she said, forcing a cheerful reply although she felt the floor was collapsing beneath her. "Must've fallen into a temporary food coma from the wine and cheesecake. Sorry, everyone."

"We'll head home soon," Scott said, smiling as he cupped her shoulder. "I know you were out in the garden all day. You're probably beat."

"Yep," she whispered, trying like hell to keep the tears from forming in her eyes.

The four of them finished dinner, Ashlyn barely saying a word as she inwardly told herself to buck up. Only one day into this new phase of her relationship with Scott and she was acting like a jilted girlfriend. It was pathetic. This thing between them was sexual, and she was a big girl. Yes, she'd felt connected to him last night as they'd made love but that was just hormones and lust. Determined to push away any other feelings, she straightened her spine and attempted to end the night on a positive note.

She chatted with Scott as they drove home, hoping like hell he hadn't noticed her embarrassing space-out session. *This is a sexual affair, Rivers, that's all. Get a fucking grip.*

Scott pulled up in front of her house and shut down the car. With a hesitant gaze, he asked, "Do you want me to come in? If not, that's fine. It was a long dinner."

Lifting her chin, Ashlyn firmed her resolve. "I'd love for you to come inside."

Giving a nod, those eyes still swirling with emotion, he hopped out to open her door.

Scott led Ashlyn inside, realizing he was about two seconds away from strangling himself. It was obvious he'd upset her with his comment about Tina, and he was frustrated at his idiocy. Since he hadn't been with anyone since the accident, he'd never had to censor his comments about Tina. Although what he'd said was true, he could only imagine how difficult it was for Ashlyn to hear. If he'd been thinking at all, he never would've said it. Cursing himself, he hung his jacket on her hook before following her to the living room.

"Man, that wine was great but I'm beat," she said, falling onto the plushy couch. "Be honest. How much did you hate the meatloaf?"

Sitting beside her, he grimaced. "It was terrible. I think most of it went into my napkin."

Leaning her head against the back of the couch, she smiled. "I saw that. You were pretty sly though. I don't think they noticed."

"I hope not. I feel bad but realize yours is the only meatloaf I would ever consider eating."

Chuckling, she toed off her boots and shimmied off her socks before tucking her feet underneath her legs. Sideways on the couch, with her back against the arm, she looked content and sleepy. Thankful some of her worries seemed to have dissipated, he encircled her ankles and lifted her feet over his thighs. With strong movements, he began to massage her feet, feeling himself harden at the sight of her cute painted toenails.

"Oh, man, if you keep that up, there won't be any banging tonight," she said, eyes drooping as she relaxed into the cushions. "And that's our primary purpose here, mister."

His eyes roved over her as his hands worked their magic. "It's not my only purpose, Ashlyn," he said, wanting so badly to undo the damage. "I love spending time with you, even if we don't have sex. You understand that, right?"

"Mmm-hmm..." she said, although her gaze was wary.

"I'm really sorry about what I said—"

Holding up a hand, she cut him off. "You have nothing to be sorry for. I think it's amazing you talk about your wife that way. One day, I swear I'll find someone who talks about me that way. It gives me hope."

Scott found the words extremely sad while also struggling with the fact he didn't want to live in a world where another man spoke about Ashlyn that way. *Ever*. Although it made him a selfish bastard, he wanted her all to himself, even though he wasn't anywhere near ready to offer her those words.

Inwardly sighing, he understood that keeping this thing between them purely sexual was unlikely. He was enamored with her—her tenacious spirit, her generous heart, and her glorious smile—and she seemed pretty caught up in him too, judging by her reaction to his careless words earlier that evening. Fear coursed through him as he contemplated how quickly things could get messy.

And yet, along with the fear, there was a sense of...anticipation? Excitement? He didn't know how to categorize the swirling feelings but knew what he'd found with Ashlyn was special. A connection like theirs didn't come along often and he didn't want to squander it by being a coward or staying stuck in the past.

"I'm so honored to be with you," he almost whispered, wishing he could give her more. "If I didn't want to punch your ex in the face so badly, I'd find him and thank him for helping you find your way here."

"Aw," she said, biting her lip. "That's really cute. If you ever meet him, you have my permission to pound his face in."

"Noted." Dying to touch her more intimately, he rested her feet against the back of the couch before kicking off his shoes. Stretching over her, he settled his aching body between her thighs, thrilled when she encircled him with her arms.

"I had a good time tonight," he said, kissing her softly as he cradled her head atop the couch arm. "Thank you for coming with me."

"Thank you for inviting me," she said, reaching up to steal another kiss. "Now be a good contractor and put those skillful hands to use."

Scott wanted nothing more than to make love to her, but he still worried she was hurting. Gliding his fingers over her cheek, he asked, "Are you sure? I'm okay just kissing you, honey."

"Make out with me for a while," she said, tugging him closer, "then you can ravish me. Sound good?" She waggled her eyebrows.

"Sounds amazing." Enveloping her in a torrid kiss, he followed her command and lost himself in her arms. Later, as he drove home on the darkened street, he vowed to consider his words more carefully in the future. Hurting Ashlyn had ripped open something deep inside his heart that was painful and raw, and he was determined never to do it again.

Chapter 16

The permits were approved the next week, and Ashlyn settled in for a long spring and summer where her house would be occupied by three very nice—and very hungry—contractors. She found Dan, Caleb, and Larry charming but by the second day, they'd consumed every snack she'd offered them. Studying her sparse fridge, Ashlyn decided to use it as a test of sorts. She would make different meals and appetizers for them and get much-needed feedback on what to offer from her food truck. All in all, a win-win.

She and Scott still ran most mornings but decided not to sleep together during the week. Since they wanted to keep things light, they felt it was best to only engage in the sexual aspect of their relationship on the weekends. It was a relief to Ashlyn since she was still thrown by Scott's words, although she tried like hell not to be affected. His heartfelt statement about his wife was evidence of what they both knew deep within: their time together was temporary.

Sure, they would still be friends when their sexual relationship ended, but they would never share the intimacy Ashlyn was beginning to crave deep in her soul. Every time they made love, Scott would look at her with those melted brown eyes, causing her to wish for things that could never be.

No, this time, she had to be a realist. The disaster with Robert had proven that. Ashlyn wanted it all one day: a husband who adored her, little rug rats who could run around in her garden, and maybe even a few pets to top it off. As she'd told Scott, she wanted the fairy tale. To find a man who would love her to distraction and vow she was the one he cherished above all others.

Scott had found his one true love, and she'd been ripped away from him, along with their daughter. As her sentiment for him grew, she understood how seriously he'd taken his promises to Tina. She didn't begrudge him for it and certainly didn't blame him, but he wouldn't be her soulmate. No matter how badly a tiny corner of her heart wished it could possibly happen.

Knowing that, Ashlyn strove to keep the relationship fun and airy, deciding that if it was purely sexual, they could at least knock each other's socks off. After all, Scott was *hot* and sex with him was a thousand times better than with Robert, or anyone else she'd ever been with, for that matter. His attraction for her was evident, giving her a much-needed confidence boost, and she reveled in his smoldering kisses and words of desire every time he touched her heated skin. He was extremely attentive, making sure she reached her peak each time before he took his own pleasure. In contrast, by the end of her sexual relationship with Robert, she'd been all but convinced he'd forgotten where her clit was.

Enveloped in her newfound sexual prowess, she wanted to offer him a chance to experience the same. After all, he'd been celibate for almost six years. The man had to have a million fantasies, and she was determined to help him experience as many as possible before their time together ended.

One night, two weeks after dinner with the Robinsons, Ashlyn was curved into Scott's side on her couch as they watched a movie. She'd cooked a quiche, which they'd devoured, and he'd suggested the movie afterward.

"I thought you might want to work off the quiche," she said, arching a brow as she wiped the table clean.

"We can do that after the movie. I feel like I come here every weekend and you cook for me and then we have sex."

"Yes," she said slowly, her tone teasing. "I'm pretty sure that's our arrangement."

Stepping forward, he cupped her shoulders, causing her to stare into his eyes. "I'm getting all the perks here, Ash," he said, the nickname slipping from his lips. He'd started calling her that somewhere along the way and it made her insides tingle each time he spoke the word in his deep baritone. "Don't get me wrong, I love it, but I want to make you feel special too."

"Are you under the impression I'm not enjoying myself? If so, your radar is *really* off."

Chuckling, he gripped her arms. "So am I, but I want to hold you. Hang for a bit without it being about sex. Maybe give you a kick-ass shoulder massage?"

"Well, hot damn," she said, trailing to the sink and washing her hands. "I'll never turn down a massage."

They'd trailed to the living room where they'd decided on a Netflix movie and she'd sat on the floor between his legs as he massaged her into heaven. Somewhere along the way, she'd lost her shirt, but her bra had remained...for the moment. Afterward, she'd crawled onto the couch and snuggled into his body, feeling so content when he'd wrapped the blanket around her and held her close.

Now that the movie had ended, she clicked off the TV and gazed up at him as he stroked her bare arm.

"That was good," he said, brushing a tendril of hair off her forehead. "It was cool to see Chris Evans as a bad guy for once."

"Mmm-hmm..." was her quiet reply as the wheels in her mind turned. Deciding to go for it, she blurted the question on her mind. "What are you into, Scott? I mean, sex with you is awesome but I don't feel like we're taking full advantage of this 'purely sexual' thing we've entered into." She made quotation marks with her fingers.

Something flashed in his eyes, perhaps anger, and she continued before he could argue. He was always quick to insist their relationship wasn't merely sexual, which she assumed stemmed from his chivalrous nature, but Ashlyn understood and accepted the terms they'd set.

"Come on," she said, shimmying against him, loving how his body hardened. "There have to be things you want to try. This is the perfect opportunity to experiment."

Those gorgeous eyes roved over her face as he considered. "I watched a lot of porn over the past few years," he said, grimacing.

"Ohhh, kinky."

"It's not that great. Believe me. No woman gets that excited from one touch or caress."

"I got pretty excited from your massage." She waggled her eyebrows.

Laughing, he threaded his fingers through her hair. "It makes me insanely happy to hear that. Anyway, I found myself really drawn to..."

"Yes?" she said, batting her eyelashes, finding his slight blush adorable.

"I'm afraid you're going to think I'm weird."

"No way. I'll tell you my fantasies if you tell me yours."

"Damn, I can't pass up that offer." Tightening his fingers in her hair, he gently tugged. "This," he murmured, lust simmering in his expression. "Bondage. Dominance. It really turned me on for some reason."

Ashlyn arched into his grip, the reaction natural. Sensual. "That makes a lot of sense."

"Yeah?"

Nodding, she slid her arms around his neck. "Control has been taken from you in very important moments of your life. It makes sense you'd look for ways to reclaim it."

His sexy smile made her insides tingle.

"What's so funny?"

"Nothing. It's just amazing how well you read me. I feel such a connection with you, Ashlyn. I never expected it."

"Well, let's connect, then," she said, drawing him closer and bringing his mouth to hers so she wouldn't have to look at the admiration in his eyes. Her heart wanted to see it as something more. Something that meant feelings and emotion, and she was determined to shut those yearning down. Scott's tongue battled with hers, setting the exposed skin of her torso on fire. Needing more, she drew back.

"What if I got on my knees and you tied my hands behind my back before I sucked you?"

His muscled frame shuddered. "You'd do that?"

"Hell yes."

"Wait." His eyebrows drew together. "What's your fantasy?"

Biting her lip, she deliberated. She had a lot of fantasies but figured she'd stick to one that was relatively safe. "You could blindfold me while I'm bound."

"That's your biggest fantasy?" he asked in a droll tone.

"I'm working my way up," she teased, kissing him before she rose from the couch. "Be right back."

After trailing up the stairs and grabbing two scarves, she headed back down and walked to stand between his legs. "You can tie my hands with this one and blindfold me with this one."

Placing his hands on her waist, he slid them over her jeans, lowering the zipper before gliding them down her legs. Stepping out, she waited, clad in her bra and panties while he gazed at her.

"You're so pretty, honey," he said, sliding his palm over her abdomen, causing the muscles to quiver. "Sometimes, when I touch you, I think I'm stuck in a dream."

Pulling him to stand, she extended the scarves. "Well, let's make it a fucking reality."

His resulting laugh was so open and free, spurring a sense of happiness in her bones since he'd experienced so much heartache. If she could make him laugh like that forever, it wouldn't be enough. Somehow, in the few months she'd known Scott, making him happy had become one of her greatest sources of joy.

"Come on," she said, tugging him to the soft carpet atop the hardwood floor. "Let's show the internet how it's done."

"You're amazing," he whispered before grasping her wrist and turning her to face the fireplace. A flash of fabric flitted across the corner of her gaze as he threw the scarves over his shoulder. Lightly grazing his fingers over her shoulder blades, she hissed as he unclasped her bra, the chilly air making her exposed nipples tighten.

Sliding his hands around, he cupped them and gently pinched the tight buds. "Are you wet?" he whispered in her ear.

"Yes."

"Let me taste."

Shivering from the deep command, she guided her hand under the lacy underwear, finding her wet center with her index finger.

Circling it through the moisture, she gathered it until it drenched her skin. Lifting her hand, she held it high, touching her fingertip to Scott's lips as his chin rested on her shoulder.

"Mmmm..." he groaned, rubbing his lips over the wetness before opening them and sliding over her finger. Gaze cemented to hers, he sucked her dry, moaning as he jutted his jean-covered erection into her lower back.

"Scott..."

"Let me slide off those sexy panties, honey." Kneeling, he hooked his fingers around the fabric and slid them down her legs, tossing them aside. Turning her to face him, he tugged off his shirt before lifting her leg over his shoulder. "Hold on to my shoulders."

Grasping on for dear life, Ashlyn threw her head back as he drew her close, burying his face in the sopping center. His tongue was magic as it slid over her swollen folds, down to her opening, before plunging inside her in a maddening rhythm. Feeling her balance waver, she dug her nails into his skin, clutching so she wouldn't fall.

Scott growled at the gesture, pushing his face further into her core before trailing his tongue higher to flick her clit. Sucking the engorged nub into his mouth, he milked her, the sensation so pleasurable against the nerve-filled bud. Feeling the climax on the horizon, she thought she might collapse.

But he was there, as he always seemed to be, his broad hands gripping her hips and providing the anchor she needed. Trusting him to hold her high, she gave over to the orgasm. Tossing her head back, she screamed, the sound frenzied and ragged. Tiny pinpricks of pleasure exploded in every cell as stars burst behind her eyelids. Lost to the intense feeling, she began to laugh, overcome with bliss.

"This was supposed to be *your* fantasy," she said as she panted.

"Oh, it is," was his sensual reply. Standing, he slid one of the scarves from his shoulder and placed it over her eyes, tying it behind her head. "Is that good?"

"Mmm-hmm..." Ashlyn said, the deep timbre of his voice even more pronounced through the darkness.

She heard rustling as he removed his clothes and felt his body brush hers as he maneuvered behind her. The silk of the scarf trailed over her wrists as he bound them, causing her body to grow taut. He trailed back around, the tips of his fingers caressing her quivering stomach as he moved. Cupping her shoulders, he gently urged her to balance on her knees. The carpet was soft beneath her and Ashlyn waited, her breath shallow as she gave him all control.

"You're so damn beautiful, Ash," he said, sliding her hair from underneath the scarf so it fell silky down her shoulders. It would give him a stronghold and she was ready to feel his broad hands tug the tresses.

"Don't go easy on me," she said, licking her lips, ensuring they were glistening. "I don't give up control easily but this is really turning me on."

His breathy laugh washed over her. "I've never been so turned on in my fucking life."

The words were meaningful, even if they were said in the throes of passion. Perhaps once this was over, he would at least remember her as the woman he'd cared about enough to reclaim this part of himself. Something she could give him that was theirs alone. Tilting her head, she whispered, "Come here," and opened her lips wide.

Scott touched the smooth flesh of his cock to her mouth, circling the head over her wet, swollen lips. Enflamed and ready, she closed them over his straining skin. He cursed above her, threading his fingers through her hair and gripping tightly. Dying to take him to heaven, she began to move, sliding her mouth over his engorged length.

He began to jut inside the warm depths and she met his thrusts with her tongue, licking and bathing his flesh as he groaned. Reveling in the taste of his salty essence, she gave over to his undulating hips, letting him work his cock into the confines of her mouth.

The broad head of his cock reached her throat and she relaxed, willing to let him test and play with her. Opening herself to him this way was so damn freeing, and she realized how special it was that she could trust a man so completely after her most recent betrayal. Scott had given her that gift, and she cherished it, as she cherished so many things in their short time together.

Strong fingers tightened at her scalp and he whispered dirty words to her as his body hammered into hers. "I'm close, honey," he rasped. "Do you want me to pull out?"

She shook her head around him, and he received the message loud and clear, judging by his resulting groan. Fists tightened to the point of pleasure-pain in her hair as he pounded her wet mouth. For a moment, he stilled and called her name before jets of his release pulsed against the back of her throat. Open and raw, she swallowed his essence; his smooth, taut skin throbbing. When he eventually stilled, she felt giddy and replete. He stroked her temple as his softening shaft sat between her lips, causing her to smile around him.

"Well, I'm dead," he teased above her.

Laughing, she tightened her lips and sucked him again for good measure, causing him to shudder. "Good grief. You're insatiable." Pulling himself from her mouth, he grazed his fingers across the curve of her jaw.

"Better than internet porn?"

Chuckling, he kneeled before her. She sensed his movements as he reached behind and untied her bound wrists. "So much better." He slid the blindfold from her head, tossing it to the floor before palming her cheeks. Brown eyes swam with sated desire as he contemplated her. "You're incredible."

"Oh, that's just the beginning, buddy. We've got a whole list of fantasies to work through."

"Can't fucking wait."

Sliding his arm under the backs of her knees, he lifted her and she gave a little yelp as he carried her toward the couch. Lowering, he sprawled her over his chest before pulling the blanket to cover their cooling skin. "I need to hold you," he murmured, combing his fingers through her hair.

Nodding, she laid her cheek on his chest and snuggled into him, figuring it wouldn't hurt to cuddle a bit. As her heartbeat against his, their combined rhythm strong and entwined, she understood she was balancing on a dangerous precipice. Falling in love was not on her agenda. At least, not until she got her life in order. The renovations needed to be finished and her business needed to be established before she even considered getting serious with anyone. There wasn't room for anything else in her life right now.

Scott shifted below her, pulling her tighter, and her heart slammed inside her chest. *Do **not** fall in love with a man who is incapable of loving you back, Ashlyn.* The words filtered through her mind but, deep in her soul, she already knew she was doomed.

Chapter 17

♥

Scott examined the finishes in Ashlyn's main bathroom, pleased with the work. His contractors had done a fantastic job and had now moved onto the second bathroom. They'd also pulled out the old fireplace and replaced it with a new gas one, making her living room appear more modern. It would be a nice touch for people who took the haunted homes tour.

Ashlyn was in town now, meeting with Chad Hanson and Lance Downey, the county's health commissioner, regarding the various permits she would need for her food truck. His lips curved as he imagined her shaking them down for discounts on the permits and asking them to fast-track the approvals. Could you even get a discount on a permit fee? Scott wasn't sure, but if anyone could, it was the firecracker of a woman who seemed to consume his every thought lately.

Becoming involved with Ashlyn sexually had added another layer to their budding friendship, and he became more thankful for her every day. Her openness was slowly healing something inside he hadn't realized was still broken. After all the therapy he'd slogged through, he thought he was relatively healed, but he'd never really considered the very last step: moving on and allowing himself to care for someone. Perhaps even getting married again and starting a family.

The idea was daunting and sent shards of sticky, uncomfortable emotion through his veins every time he contemplated it. The notion of having a family again had always been there but it had been...*distant*. As long as it remained far away, it wasn't real. But sometimes, when Ashlyn would flash one of her beaming smiles, he would feel pangs of longing in his gut. He couldn't quite visualize the longing but knew he was headed down the path of wanting something more with her.

Closing his eyes, Scott pushed the thoughts away, telling himself he had ample time to reconcile them. For now, he could only fathom staying casual and Ashlyn seemed to feel the same. In fact, she vocalized it quite often. For some reason, her insistence their relationship was purely sexual bothered him. Yes, they'd agreed to keep it light but he also felt an intense connection with her. Didn't she feel it too?

Sighing, he berated himself for wanting it both ways. What they had was amazing and overthinking it would just murk the waters. For now, he was content to be with her in their current capacity. Hell, he was more than content. Elated, in fact. Ashlyn made him so damn happy.

After finishing the inspection, he trailed down her porch stairs and into his car before dialing Peter.

"Hey, Scott," his friend said over the Bluetooth. "I'm just finishing my review of the Kingsley contract. Everything looks great. I'm going to send it to Mark for final review," he said, referencing the local attorney they both used.

"Perfect," Scott said, amazed at how many things were going right in his life for once. "I'm so happy we got that job. It sets the firm up nicely for the next year and beyond."

"You've got a thriving business, my friend. I should've known when you left me in the dust during woodshop class in high school. And I mean the literal dust. I had no idea what I was doing."

"You had other talents. Speaking of, Ashlyn's a big fan of karaoke. I want to surprise her and take her to karaoke night at the pub. I'm hoping you and Carrie will come and save me with your awesome duets."

Silence stretched over the Bluetooth. "Peter?"

"Sorry, I'm just a bit floored by the fact that my stoic friend is now begging me to do karaoke. Carrie and I have asked you to come to karaoke night a hundred times."

"I know," Scott said, rolling his eyes. "I convinced myself I hated it. But, if Ashlyn loves it, I'm in."

"Wow, man. You're really into her."

"I'm pretty into her," Scott said. "And the whole 'keep it light' thing is great but I want to show her it doesn't have to be completely sexual. She says karaoke is one of her favorite things so I'll suck it up and go if it makes her smile."

"Sounds like you've got yourself a girlfriend."

"No labels, Peter. Just two adults having fun. I didn't realize how much I needed this and I think she did too. Sounds like her ex was a huge asshole. I'm determined to make her forget he even existed."

"Well, I'll talk to Carrie and make sure she has a babysitter for Wednesday night. This is going to be fun."

Once the call was ended, Scott dialed Ashlyn.

"You're calling to tell me the bathroom looks perfect, right?" she said across the Bluetooth.

"It looks amazing. The second bathroom should be done by the end of next week and then they'll move to the den. The guys love you, by the way."

"I've bought their affection with food and I'm not ashamed," was her cheerful reply, causing him to laugh.

"Smart woman. They're working faster than I've ever seen. They want to do a good job for you."

"So?" she asked as he heard her start her ignition. "What's up? Besides your contractors being awesome?"

"Are you free on Wednesday night? I want to take you somewhere. It's a surprise. Peter and Carrie will be there too."

"Ohhh, a surprise. I love those. Are we sanctioning a weeknight together though?"

"Yes, and it can be completely platonic if you want. I think you're going to love it."

"Well, now I'm intrigued. What time should I be ready and what should I wear?"

"I'll pick you up at seven and something casual."

"I'll be ready. Oh, and Scott?"

"Hmmm?"

"If I really like it, I might break our no banging on a weekday rule afterward. Ta ta!"

The phone clicked off as he chuckled. Damn, he'd laughed more since she'd come into his life than he had in years. Grateful for her, he filtered through his mind, trying like hell to think of a song he could sing on Wednesday that wouldn't make everyone's eardrums bleed.

Ashlyn told herself not to break into a full-on run down the porch stairs when Scott pulled up on Wednesday. Their week had been busy and they hadn't been able to do their morning runs so she hadn't seen him since Sunday. Only a few days, but it had seemed like a lifetime.

"Hey," she said, jumping in the passenger seat before he could exit the car.

"I would've opened your door."

Leaning over, she gave him a peck on the lips. "I know, but this was faster. I'm excited to get on with this amazing surprise."

He gave her a cheeky, adorable grin before driving them into town and parking in front of the pub. "We're going to the pub?"

"Yep," he said, walking around and opening her door. "Come on."

Following him inside, she noticed the banner hanging above the stage that sat in the back corner. It read "Karaoke Night" and her heart damn near exploded. "No way! *You* do karaoke?"

"I do karaoke *very* badly, but Peter and Carrie are pretty much rock stars. They've agreed to meet us so I don't embarrass us too badly."

"Oh my god," she said, approaching the table closest to the stage. "I used to do karaoke all the time in Manhattan. Let's grab this table. I need to see *everything*."

Terry sauntered over, a sparkle in her eyes. "Well, well. If it isn't Scott Grillo here on karaoke night. I'm about to call the police and tell them your body has been invaded by aliens."

"I'm here to make Ashlyn happy," Scott said, holding his hands up and showing his palms. "I *might* sing if the mood strikes. We'll see."

"Uh-huh," she said, eyeing them both. "Vodka soda, honey?" she asked Ashlyn.

"Yes, please."

"You gonna have a real drink tonight?" she asked Scott. "Might need one for karaoke."

"Just the usual," he said. "Gotta be able to focus on the lyrics."

Terry arched a brow. "I'll believe it when I see it. Be right back, guys."

They sat at the four-top table, Carrie and Peter joining them a few minutes later. The karaoke DJ showed up and assembled his equipment on the stage before dropping two large books on the table.

"This one's by artist and this one's by song," he said, pointing at the songbooks. "Just write the number and song title on the request forms and we'll get you in."

"We're totally doing that Rihanna and Mikky Echo duet," Carrie said to Peter.

His eyes narrowed as he considered. "It's not really my style, but I'll do it for you, Care Bear."

She flashed a smile and Ashlyn noticed their easy affection with each other. Suddenly dying to know their story, she made a mental note to grill Scott as soon as she had an opportunity. They stood up to sing their first duet and Ashlyn's eyes widened.

"Good grief, they're amazing!" she said to Scott as he sat beside her.

"Yep," he said, nodding. "Carrie is the preacher's daughter and learned to sing in church. Peter joined the choir until her dad kicked him out in tenth grade."

"Why did her dad kick him out?"

"Because he realized Peter only joined to do private sessions with his daughter."

"No way! I thought I saw a spark between them. Tell me everything."

Laughing, he took a sip of his drink. "It's a long, sordid story. What isn't when you've been around the block a few times? In my opinion, they were always meant for each other but had a bit of a star-crossed lovers thing going on."

Ashlyn observed them onstage, staring into each other's eyes as they sang the duet. "How sad. They could be together now, right? I mean, her divorce is final, isn't it?"

"Yeah," Scott said, shrugging. "They still fight it for some reason. I've never really understood it. I mean, they both had struggles but have entered new phases of their lives. They say they've let go of the past but it's easier said than done." His expression grew sad and she wondered if he was still speaking about Peter and Carrie.

"Well, I'm ready for my song," she said, hoping to change his forlorn expression. "I'm going to kill it for my Ardor Creek debut. Just you wait."

Once Peter and Carrie finished their song, complete with raucous applause from the other twenty or so patrons in the bar, Ashlyn handed over her request. Taking the mic, she belted out one of her go-to songs, Midnight Train to Georgia by Gladys Knight and the Pips. She'd always been pretty confident about her voice and knew this one was a winner. When she was finished, she was met with cheers and whistles from some of the old regulars sitting at the bar. Giving a bow, she basked in the praise.

"Wow, you weren't kidding," Scott said when she sat down. "You're awesome. I'm pretty intimidated."

"Don't be," she said, taken by his compliment. "It's all about having fun, right?"

And boy, did she have fun the rest of the night. She sang a few duets with Carrie and one with Peter before Scott reluctantly agreed to sing Don't Let the Sun Go Down on Me with her. He wasn't half bad and only seemed slightly embarrassed when it was over.

As the DJ broke down his equipment, the four of them waited for Terry to bring the check as they finished their drinks.

"This was so fun, guys," Ashlyn said, lifting her glass. "Thank you for showing this newbie a great time."

"You're family now, honey," Carrie said as they all clinked their glasses. "A few months in Ardor Creek is all it takes. Welcome home."

The poignant words melted her heart and she felt the prick of tears. "I'm so lucky to have found you all. Thank goodness I stalked Scott. I've never had a bad result from stalking if I tried long enough."

"I'm happy you didn't give up," Scott said, squeezing her wrist. Carrie and Peter exchanged a look at the sweet gesture and Ashlyn figured that was her cue to get things moving. As fun as this was, it was now venturing into double date territory, and she and Scott weren't on that level.

"Well, I'm glad you drove," she said to Scott. "I'm a bit plowed. Ready to blow this joint?"

After a round of hugs and goodbyes, Scott drove her home and held her hand as he walked her inside.

"I'm perfectly capable of walking up the stairs, Scott. I'm drunk but not *that* drunk."

"I know," he said, closing the door behind him as they stood in her foyer. "But it was an excuse to hold your hand."

God, he was so adorable as he smiled down at her in the dim light. How could anyone resist that perfect, sexy smile? "If you want to break our no banging on the weekdays rule, I'm down to make an exception tonight." She waggled her eyebrows.

"I'd be a fool to turn that down," he said, tucking a silky strand of hair behind her ear, "but I don't mind waiting until Friday either. I didn't take you out to get anything in return."

"I know you didn't," she said, tugging his wrist. "Come on." They began to walk up the stairs.

"We always hang at your house, which is fine," he said as they entered her bedroom, "but I want to have you over to my place. You haven't even seen it and we've been hanging out for a while now."

Ashlyn struggled to keep her expression impassive. She'd known this topic was going to come up eventually and had tried like hell to avoid it. Something about being with Scott in his home, where he'd lived with his wife and daughter, made her feel uncomfortable.

Should she tell him? Were her feelings misplaced or ridiculous? She honestly had no idea and it made her feel off-balance.

"Want to come over on Friday?" he asked, unbuttoning his shirt before tossing it on the chair. "I have to go to Scranton to visit an investor and there's a fantastic sushi restaurant I can get take out from. Not as great as Manhattan, I'm sure, but it's the best sushi you'll get within seventy miles of Ardor Creek."

Ashlyn gnawed her lip, contemplating. Understanding she'd have to see his house at some point, she capitulated. "Okay, let's do it. I'll come over at seven?"

"Perfect," he murmured, stepping close to rub her bare arms now that she'd removed her shirt. "Did you have fun tonight?"

Encircling his neck, she nodded. "So much fun. Thank you, Scott."

"You make me smile, Ashlyn," he said, the words almost a whisper. "It's been a long time since anyone's done that. I hope I can make you half as happy as you make me."

Aaaaaand, now her heart was a melted pile of slush. If he only knew what he did to her when he said things like that. "You make me happy too," she whispered, rising to her toes to capture his lips. "Now bang me before I pass out."

Breaking into a laugh, he captured her lips. "Yes, ma'am."

He loved her, skillful and slow until she fell asleep in his arms. When morning came, she reached for him, knowing he wouldn't be there but wishing all the same. Ashlyn had fallen into the trap of wishing for several things lately. Things that were sure to break her heart wide open. Since she'd survived several broken hearts before, she figured one more wouldn't be so bad. After all, if you were going to rip your soul apart, might as well go down swinging.

Chapter 18

Friday arrived, along with a huge storm that had barreled up the coast during the week, threatening rain and possible tornadoes. It was now late June, and strong thunderstorms were always possible this time of year, and the residents of Ardor Creek were prepared. Noticing the half-empty shelves at the grocery store on Friday morning, Ashlyn purchased enough food for a week, just in case.

Worried for Scott since he was driving to Scranton, she shot him a text telling him not to rush home. It was better to be safe than on time. *And, if he's late, you can shave an hour off spending time in the home he built for his family.* Annoyed at the inner dialogue, she shut it off as she headed to the bank to procure a cashier's check.

She'd finally decided on the perfect food truck, which she'd found online from a married couple who'd sold produce from their farm out of the truck for many years. Ashlyn would need to install some updated appliances and give it a fresh paint job, but felt it a fortuitous find. Something about it called to her, and since it had been run by the nice, loving couple who was now retiring, she felt it had good karma built in. She'd cut the cashier's check today and would take an Uber next week to pick it up. That, combined with her home's acceptance on the haunted homes tour, now cemented her established life in Ardor Creek.

"Whether you like it or not, you're stuck here now, Ashlyn," she said as she drove to the bank. Smiling at herself in the rearview mirror, she decided being stuck in the town she was coming to adore was pretty damn awesome.

That evening, she spent extra time getting ready. It was probably silly but she wanted to look like a million bucks when she entered Scott's home. Perhaps the sexy makeup she adorned was an extra layer of protection. Regardless, she clutched onto her inner confidence and drove to his house.

Pulling into the driveway, she noticed how simple and pristine the design of the two-story home was. Ashlyn would expect nothing less from her detailed contractor. Climbing the white front porch stairs, she knocked on the door.

"Hey," Scott said, flashing a smile as he pulled it open. "You made it in between bouts of pouring rain. Nice job."

"Did you hit any of the swells when you were driving?"

"Yes, but I still managed to procure the sushi." He waggled his brows. "It's in the fridge now. If you're starving, I can grab it, or I can give you a tour first."

"A tour sounds lovely."

Sliding his palm over hers, he interlaced their fingers. "Let's start here."

Scott tugged her into the living room, which had the standard couch, chair, TV, and other functional items. A large mantel set atop his fireplace, lined with multiple picture frames. She listened with half an ear as he detailed her on the bay window, dying to see the pictures of Tina and Ella. Finally, he led her to the mantel and she gazed upon the photos.

Pulling her hand from his, she ran her finger over one with an image of Scott, a pretty woman with long brown hair and a smiling toddler with a smattering of brown curls. "They're both so beautiful."

"They were," he said softly, staring at the photo. "I keep the pictures up so I remember their faces. I'd started to forget a few years after the accident and my therapist said it was a good way to remember."

Swallowing thickly, she nodded. "Makes sense." Lowering her hand, she looked over the other ones. "Who's this?"

"Those are my parents. They both passed away several years ago. That's Tina's mom," he said, pointing to a picture of a woman holding Ella. "She lives in Scranton and I try to keep in touch but it's not easy."

"Life gets in the way," Ashlyn said, giving a sympathetic smile.

Something flashed across his features she couldn't decipher. "That and other things. Anyway, I wanted you to see what they look like. That's probably weird but you're really important to me, Ashlyn, and...I don't know...I just wanted you to see the people who meant so much to me."

"I get it," she said, re-lacing their fingers and squeezing. "I'm honored you want to share that part of yourself with me."

His eyes darted between hers. "I'm beginning to think I don't deserve you," he whispered, cupping her cheek with his free hand. "How in the hell are you so understanding?"

"I've had my share of loss too," she said, shrugging. "Losing Grandma Jean was hard and explaining to everyone that my fiancé jilted me for some skank wasn't easy."

"Actually, I think *you* jilted *him*," he said, arching a brow.

"After he stuck his dick in someone else," she muttered. Sighing, she shook her head. "Anyway, I was curious about them and I'm happy you feel comfortable enough to show me these." She gestured to the pictures. "I'm excited for the rest of the tour."

Tugging her through the house, he showed her the kitchen before trailing upstairs to show her the bedrooms. Ella's room was clean but lined with all the trappings of a little girl's abode: pink princess canopied bed, stuffed animals, books. Ashlyn took it all in, wondering if he planned to leave it like that forever.

"My therapist said to leave it this way until I was ready to let go." His gaze scanned the room, pensive and sad. "I just haven't been ready yet."

"Everything happens when it's meant to be," she said, unable to comprehend losing a child. The agony must be devastating. He led her into the master bedroom, which was clean and tidy, as she'd come to expect from Scott.

"Love the four-poster bed," she said, waggling her eyebrows. "You could tie someone to that puppy and live out all your bondage fantasies."

Chuckling, he nodded. "I bought it a few months after the accident. Our old bed was a wedding gift from Tina's grandmother and I had trouble sleeping in it."

Well, at least she wouldn't have to bang him in the bed he'd shared with his wife. Ashlyn was pretty understanding but there was no way in hell she'd be able to get a lady boner in his wife's grandmother's bed. *Ever.*

"That's a thoughtful gift. Is her Grandma still alive?"

"No, she passed a few years ago. Tina was an only child and her mom is the only one left on her side of the family. She married a man in Scranton after Tina graduated high school and once her father died."

"Got it," Ashlyn said, suddenly ready to exit the room where he'd spent so much intimate time with his wife. She certainly didn't begrudge or resent him for it but, still, it felt...*weird.* Like she was the other woman or something. After Robert's betrayal, she wanted to be as far removed from that sentiment as possible.

"Well, I think I'm ready for sushi," she said, beaming up at him. "I hope you got spicy tuna. It's my favorite."

"I damn near bought the whole restaurant," he said, leading her back downstairs. "Let's dig in."

Giving herself a silent pep-talk to stay in the moment and enjoy their time together, she followed him to the kitchen to enjoy the sushi.

Scott had a fantastic time with Ashlyn as they devoured the sushi. Awed by her empathetic and understanding nature, he felt extremely connected to her as they laughed and told each other stories from their pasts. He'd felt compelled to show her the pictures of Tina and Ella, somehow craving her reaction. He didn't want to make her feel uncomfortable, although that was probably inevitable. But she'd come to mean so much to him in the months they'd known each other and he wanted her to know the other two people who'd comprised his life for so long.

She'd reacted with such grace, causing him to wonder how he would feel if the situations were reversed. Honestly, he couldn't say he would react with such calm acceptance if she thrust pictures in his face of someone she'd loved and shared the same intimacies with. Trying to be completely honest with himself, he realized it would hurt, deep in his heart where he'd come to hold so much sentiment for her. As they finished up the sushi, he searched her expression for any signs of hesitancy, finding none. Either she was an excellent actress or perhaps it truly didn't bother her. If not, he admired her fortitude.

After dinner, they settled in on the couch to watch a Netflix show. Eventually, their cuddles turned to caresses and they made love on the soft leather. Sated and sanguine, they fell asleep on the couch before a huge clap of thunder startled them both awake.

"Holy shit," Ashlyn said, sliding off the couch and beginning to don her clothes as lightning flashes illuminated her silhouette in the darkness. "This storm means business."

Scott tossed off the blanket and rose, sliding on his boxer briefs before walking to the window. Rain pelted the ground and he also observed some rather large hailstones. Worried for her safety, he turned to face her. "I don't think you should drive in this."

She finished buttoning her jeans and reached for her shirt, sliding it over her head. "I'll be fine. I've driven in storms before."

"It's hailing and the trees are whipping. It looks really bad."

Sitting on the couch, she slid on her sandals. "I'm sure I'll be okay. It's cute for you to worry, though." Standing, she ran her hands over her jean-clad thighs. "Thanks so much for the sushi. It was awesome."

Approaching her, he gently gripped her upper arms, forcing her to meet his gaze. "Ashlyn," he said softly, "please. I wouldn't forgive myself if anything happened to you. Please stay with me tonight."

Her throat bobbed as she swallowed and her gaze was wary. "We agreed on no sleepovers."

His eyes darted between hers, trying to assess her mood. "I know but that was before..."

Dark eyebrows drew together over those stunning eyes. "Before what?"

Blood pulsed through his body from his pounding heart, comprehending they'd somehow stepped into a meaningful discussion they weren't prepared for. "Before I realized how much I needed you."

"Scott—"

"Please," he pleaded, squeezing her arms. "I can't send you out there tonight, Ash. I want you to be safe."

She inhaled a deep breath, pondering. Scott felt the seconds tick by as if they were centuries. Finally, she gave an almost imperceptive nod. "Okay."

Relief flooded his veins as he released the breath lodged in his lungs. "Okay."

Toying with her lip with her teeth, she contemplated him. "Can we sleep on the couch though? Is that too uncomfortable? I, um..." she rubbed her forehead with her fingers. "I don't know if this is fair or unfair or what the hell it is, but I don't think I can sleep in the room where you slept with your wife. I'm really sorry but figure it's probably best to get that out in the open so it doesn't fester. There were a lot of things I didn't say to my ex and I'm determined to learn from that experience."

Scott's spine straightened as realization washed over him. It was perfectly natural for her to feel uncomfortable sleeping in the room he'd shared with Tina. Anxiety swamped him as he wondered if she'd felt this way the entire night. How could she not? He'd all but shoved his family in her face and just expected her to happily float along. Closing his eyes, he cursed himself for being such an oblivious idiot.

"I'm just realizing how awful this whole evening must've been for you," he said, lifting his lids to search her gaze. "God, Ashlyn, I'm such an ass. I only saw this entire experience from my perspective."

Compassion laced her features. "I'm fine, Scott. I swear. It's really meaningful that you trust me enough to let me into the home you shared with your family and to discuss them with me so openly. I hope you know that."

"But it's really fucking insensitive to what we have. I get that now. I'm so sorry."

"We agreed on terms, and I knew what I was signing up for. Please don't beat yourself up. I just want to make sure we continue to be honest with each other."

"Then be honest with me. Is this why we always hang at your house? Do you prefer we spend time together there?"

After a moment, she nodded. "Yes. Not because I don't want to know this part of you but because I think it's just easier. I hope that makes sense."

"It makes a ton of sense. I should've realized it earlier."

"There's no playbook for this situation. We're both just doing the best we can. I think it was important for me to spend some time here. But from now on, let's keep it simple."

"Okay," he said, placing a tender kiss on her forehead. "Well, we can't go anywhere tonight so let's hunker on the couch and try to get some sleep. If that's okay with you."

Nodding, she grinned. "Sleepover sanctioned for one night only. I'm down."

"Come on," he whispered, tugging her wrist.

She slid her shirt, shoes, and jeans off before crawling atop his frame after he lay down on the couch. Nestling her head into the crook of his neck, she slowly relaxed under the soft blanket he pulled over their bodies. Stroking her hair, he felt her fall into slumber, remaining awake so he could memorize the steady cadence of her breathing. It was soothing and warm, spurring him to realize something quite profound: he wanted to hold her like this every night. Not just on the weekends. Not when they carved time out of their busy schedules. But every damn night…for the rest of his life.

Racked by the realization, Scott struggled to reconcile it as the pictures atop the mantel captured his gaze. Unsure what came next, he closed his eyes and eventually allowed himself to sleep.

Chapter 19

June bled into July as Ashlyn undertook a multitude of tasks. Between renovating her food truck, securing the permits, preparing the menu, and the construction wreaking havoc on her house, her world was a whirlwind. Oh, and there was one thing that was consuming her time: she was falling head over heels in love with her sweet, sexy contractor.

After their difficult but important discussion, and subsequent sleepover at Scott's house, they'd settled into a comfortable pattern. Although the night had been filled with some awkward moments for Ashlyn, it had also created something new in its wake. The sun had risen the next morning, ushering away the frightening storm, and her fears along with it. Scott had been so vulnerable with her when discussing his family, and also so apologetic when he'd realized her discomfort, altering something within. It had alleviated much of the fear wrapped up in her feelings for him, leaving only the emotions. The giddiness and contentment now far outweighed the trepidation, and she decided to go with it for however long their tryst lasted. She seemed to make Scott happy too and figured they both deserved it.

Their "no sleepover" rule had somehow evaporated over the weeks as well. Now, Scott spent most nights at her house, both of them admitting they'd rather be together than apart. Ashlyn found it sweet that he agreed to stay at her house and didn't push her to stay in the home that represented his past. It was a testament to his ability to move on, at his pace, and she understood that was important to him.

One day in late July, she was in her front yard cleaning the newly renovated food truck when she heard shuffling outside. The contractors had left about twenty minutes ago and she squinted in the late afternoon sun as she looked through the opening where her service counter sat. "Caleb?" she called, wondering if the contractor had left something behind. "Is that you?"

"It's me, Ash," Robert's deep voice called, sending shards of ice through her veins. "Don't be mad. I finally tracked you down when I remembered your grandma lived here."

Furious, she threw down the cloth and stepped out of the food truck. His dark hair was slicked back and perfectly coiffed, reminding her of how perfection could be conveyed, even if it wasn't real. "You're trespassing."

Rolling his eyes, he crossed his arms and tapped his Italian-loafered foot upon the grass. "You're my fiancée, Ashlyn. Enough is enough. It's time we put this behind us."

"You son of a bitch," she said, pulling her phone from her back pocket. "You have two seconds before I call the cops."

"In this podunk town?" he asked, gesturing with his hands. "You can't be happy here. Come on, sweets. No one's buying it."

"My grandmother lived here and I love this place. If you knew anything about me, you'd know how much I loved visiting her here. But why would you? You never joined me on any of my visits because there was always something more important to do in the city. You never really had any interest in spending time with me, Robert. God, I can't believe I wasted four years on you."

"*You* wasted years on *me*?" he asked, incredulous. "Do you know how much embarrassment you've caused me, making me tell everyone at work and in my family our engagement is over? I told them we had a spat but you'll eventually come around."

"Still such a competent liar," she said, scoffing. "You disgust me. I have half a mind to contact everyone in your family and tell them what a cheating scumbag you are. But I won't, because that would require energy and I'm done giving you my energy, Robert. Get off my property. *Now*." Lifting the phone, she dialed 911. Before she could lift it to her ear, he knocked it out of her hand.

Stunned, she gaped at him, his features a mask of rage. They'd had terrible arguments before but she'd never actually feared him. Sticky rivulets of terror snaked up her spine as she backed away. "Are you really going to make this physical? You're better than that, Robert."

"Am I?" He stepped forward and jabbed his finger in her face. "Because you blocked me everywhere and told me what a piece of shit I am. Do you know how much that hurts, Ashlyn?"

"You *fucked* someone else!" she screamed, unable to understand how he could make *her* the bad guy in the situation. "Are you serious?"

"There are two people in every relationship. You aren't perfect, honey."

Gritting her teeth at the endearment, she lifted her chin. "But I'm not a cheater and I'm not an asshole. I'm done with whatever toxic mess we ended up in. I don't know why you insist on holding on to something that's clearly over. You need to move on."

"So you can run a dumpy food truck and live in a dilapidated house in the sticks? It's pathetic, Ash. I'm sorry I ruined your confidence but this is insane."

"You didn't ruin anything for me," she said, so furious she shoved his chest. "I'm so much better off without you—"

"Don't push me." The ominous words were said through clenched teeth as he gripped the back of her neck. "I mean it, Ashlyn—"

Suddenly, he was whipped around by an enraged Scott Grillo, who quickly proceeded to plant a crushing punch on Robert's perfect nose. Ashlyn's eyes grew wide as she heard the crunch of her former lover's cartilage, inflicted by her current lover. Thankful for his interference, she screamed Scott's name, causing him to freeze.

"He's not worth it, Scott," she said as Robert bent over, holding his bleeding nose.

Scott heaved in rapid breaths as he assessed her. "Are you okay?"

"I'm fine," she said, reaching down to pick up her phone and end the 911 call. "I didn't even hear you drive up. Holy shit."

"I figured I'd come early for the inspection," he said, lifting his fists when Robert straightened. "Don't make me hit you again."

Robert gawked at Ashlyn, wiping blood from his nose. "Really? *This* guy? You've got to be kidding me."

"*This* guy has more integrity than you have in your little finger, asshole." Pointing at his car, she demanded. "Get inside your fancy Mercedes and get the fuck out of here, Robert. That 911 call was open for at least sixty seconds. I guarantee the cops will be here any minute."

Sure enough, a cruiser appeared at the far end of the driveway, approaching as the gravel crunched beneath. Pulling to a stop, an officer stepped out and assessed the scene.

"Scott," he said with a tilt of his head. "Do I need to involve myself in this situation?"

"He assaulted me!" Robert screamed, gesturing at Scott. "I want to press charges."

The cop stayed planted in the open doorway of his car as he lazily chewed on a toothpick. "Is this true, Ms. Rivers?"

"I'll tell you one thing that's true," she said, realizing she had the opportunity to control the outcome of the situation. "This man is trespassing. I'd like to press charges against him if he doesn't leave immediately."

"Yes ma'am," the cop said with a nod. "Let me get my paperwork."

"I demand this man be arrested!" Robert yelled.

The cop walked over with a pad and pen in his hands. "I can take your statement, sir, but you'll have to give it at the station, once you've been booked on trespassing charges."

"This is absurd! She's my fiancée."

"That isn't even close to true," Ashlyn said. "However, if Mr. Torre agrees not to press assault charges against Scott, I will drop the trespassing charges."

Arching a brow, the cop said, "Sounds like a fair deal to me. What do you say, Mr. Torre."

"Fucking small-town idiots," he spat, his pristine white dress shirt now covered with blood. "Screw all of you. Hope you have a good time fucking her until you realize she's a cold-hearted bitch.

It's her fault I had to find someone else. My dick barely got hard around her toward the end—"

Scott rushed him and planted another solid punch across his cheek. Robert reeled back and Ashlyn realized he didn't know the first thing about fighting back. It made her immensely happy since he'd just landed a really hurtful verbal blow, causing a thwack in her rapidly beating heart.

"Okay, that's enough," the nice officer said, patting Scott on the shoulder. "I can let you have two but any more and I'll have to take you in. Mr. Torre, you have five seconds to get in your car and drive away before I arrest you for trespassing."

"Thanks, Gary," Scott said, clenching and unclenching his fist. Ashlyn noticed his knuckles were rapidly beginning to swell.

Robert gave them one last glare as he held his battered face. "You hicks deserve each other. Fuck this." Ambling to his car, he slammed the door and barreled down the driveway.

Rushing toward her, Scott palmed her cheeks. "Are you okay?"

"My hero," she said, trying to ease the tension. "Thank you."

"Ma'am, I can follow him if you like," Gary said.

"No," she said, shaking her head. "He doesn't deserve one speck of our energy. I appreciate your help." She extended her hand.

"Gary Lincoln," he said, shaking. "I've known this one since third grade." He gestured with his head toward Scott. "But I don't think I've seen you throw a punch that solid since Lester Goldwin tried to steal your pet turtle in middle school. Nice job, buddy."

"Lester had it coming," Scott muttered, rubbing his knuckles. "And so did that asshole."

"He seemed like a Grade A douche," Gary agreed with a tilt of his head. "Scott, make sure she has my cell in her contacts. If you ever need anything, Ms. Rivers, you let me know."

"Thank you," she said, taken by his kindness. "How did you know my name, by the way?"

"Well, I could lie and tell you I guessed who you were because I knew your grandma," he said, eyes sparkling, "but, in reality, our little town is all abuzz about your presence here, Ms. Rivers. We're all really excited about your food truck and the new addition to the haunted homes tour. But, mostly, we're all pretty stoked about how happy you've made our friend. It hasn't gone unnoticed and the locals are glad you're here."

Ashlyn's heart flooded with joy. "That's so nice of you to say. Scott is a wonderful friend."

"Uh-huh," Gary said, arching a brow. "I'm sure he is. I'll leave you all to it. Don't forget to give her my number, Scott. We need to keep your lady safe."

"Will do," Scott said as Gary trailed to the car. "Thanks, Gary."

Giving a salute, he settled into the cruiser and drove off.

"Wow," Ashlyn said, expelling a breath through puffed cheeks. "That was a *lot*."

Scott gave a sheepish grin. "Is it bad if I admit I'm glad I finally got to punch that douchebag?"

Beaming, she encircled his wrist and tugged him inside. "Not in the least. Come on, let's get some ice on that hand. And then, I'm going to make sure I thank you. While both of us are naked if you didn't catch my drift." Waggling her eyebrows, she led him to the kitchen. She prepared the ice pack and used the first aid kit to clean and bandage his knuckles.

"Man, you're fierce," she said, applying the ice to the back of his hand. "Thank god you came along when you did. Robert was never violent. I have no idea what got into him."

Lifting his free hand, Scott cupped her jaw. "Maybe he realized he pushed away the best thing that ever happened to him."

Lost in the emotion that swam in her lover's deep brown eyes, Ashlyn felt the prick of tears. "Scott..." she whispered.

"I'll never let anyone hurt you, Ashlyn. You know that right?"

Swallowing thickly, she nodded, unable to form any sort of reply since her throat was clenched tight.

Sitting there, in the kitchen that was set to be demolished and rebuilt the following week, Ashlyn felt her heart shatter. Unwilling to lie to herself any longer, she embraced the feelings that ran so deeply for the man who gazed upon her. "I'm falling for you," she whispered, shocked when a tear escaped and trailed down her cheek. "Damn it."

His lips formed a heartbreaking smile. "Sweetheart..." his tone was reverent, causing her soul to ache.

"Don't say anything back," she said, covering his lips with her fingers. "I don't want to ruin this."

"You can't ruin something as amazing as what we have," he said against her fingers. "Can you?"

"Let's not find out," she said, grinning and hoping to lift the mood. "Light and fun, remember?"

"I think we surpassed light and fun weeks ago, Ash."

Breathing a laugh, she nodded. "I think we did. But let's pretend oblivion a little while longer. At least until the house is done. I don't want to make it awkward and there's too much to contemplate. Let's discuss everything when the guys finish in September."

His eyes searched hers. "Okay. If you're sure."

"I'm sure," she said, leaning forward and placing a sweet kiss on his lips. "In the meantime, I want to cook one last magnificent meal in the oven you're going to rip away next week. What are you in the mood for?"

Eyes narrowing, he pondered. "I can't believe I'm going to say this, but I'd eat your meatloaf again. You only cooked it for me that one time."

Laughing, she bit her lip. "I didn't want to push my luck."

"I need the push sometimes," he said, rubbing his thumb over her wet cheek. "You've figured that out by now, right?"

Were they still talking about meatloaf? Ashlyn had no idea. Heeding her own request, she tabled it for later. "Note taken. Nurse that hand while I get to work."

"I'm going to inspect the second bathroom," he said, holding the pack to his knuckles as he stood. "That was the entire reason I came early today."

"Okay," she said, shooing him away. "Get to it. No slacking just because you're sleeping with the boss."

Chuckling, he kissed her forehead. "Yes, ma'am. My stuff is in the car. You'll hear me tinkering around."

Nodding, she watched his luscious backside as he walked away, wondering why she wasn't mortified she'd all but blurted out her feelings.

"Because they're true and you promised yourself complete honesty, Rivers," she mumbled to herself as she opened the fridge. "Nothing like diving right in."

Focusing on the task at hand, she got to work preparing a meatloaf that would make Scott's taste buds sing.

Chapter 20

♥

August was busy for Scott as he finalized the Kingsley contract and finished up several projects. Ashlyn finally formed her runner's group and Scott made sure to join them as often as possible. They usually ran four days a week, with Ashlyn organizing everything, mostly on Facebook. He reluctantly created an account so he could join the group and promptly realized he hated social media. How may posts could one make about politics and cats? Still, it was a nice way to connect with others and he did enjoy the updates on old friends who'd moved away from Ardor Creek.

He also began seeing his therapist again once a week, hoping to deal with some of the issues that had resurfaced due to his growing feelings for Ashlyn. He would talk to Dr. Teresa Roe about his fear of moving on and his fear of losing someone important again, amongst other things. Dr. Roe was extremely supportive and encouraged him to take some steps that signified embracing his future.

One Wednesday evening, as it poured outside his home, mimicking the tears that streamed down his cheeks, Scott began to pack up Ella's room. He left the pictures and some trinkets but gathered most of the furniture and belongings to donate to charity. He hoped they would find a loving home for another little girl and bring that family some joy.

When he was finished, he all but ached with the need to call Ashlyn.

"Hey, lover," she answered on the third ring. "Whatcha doing?"

"I, um..." Struggling with the weight of his task, he wondered how to proceed.

"Scott?"

"I'm shuffling some stuff around the house tonight," he said, running his fingers over the box that held the picture frames. He'd taken down about half the pictures on the mantel and would donate the frames as well. "It's cathartic but really heavy."

"I'll be over in ten minutes."

"You don't have to—"

"Already grabbing my keys. See you soon."

She arrived, soaking wet with a gorgeous, sympathetic smile and he showed her everything he'd boxed.

"This must be so hard," she said softly, sliding her arms around his waist. "I wish I could comfort you or experience the pain for you. I hate that you have to hurt like this."

"You've done so much, honey," he said, running his thumbs over her cheeks. "I'm so glad you're in my life."

"Me too." Lifting to her toes, she gave him a blazing kiss before they fell to the couch and held each other. Instead of the hot, sticky sex they sometimes had, Scott caressed her while placing gentle kisses across her soft skin. Eventually, they headed to her home—at his insistence even though she asserted she was fine to stay at his—and he wrapped her in his arms, spooning her as they fell asleep.

In the morning, he woke, unable to deny the truth: he was falling in love with Ashlyn. The realization was heavy and uncomfortable, and he discussed it with Dr. Roe later that week.

"Perhaps you need to ask Tina for permission to move on," Dr. Roe said, compassion in her eyes. "The act of gaining permission is very powerful."

"How do I do that?" he asked.

"You already know deep inside," she said with a soft smile. "Follow your heart, Scott."

Afterward, he'd contemplated before driving to the cemetery. He usually visited the gravesites on Sundays but felt compelled to visit them after his discussion with Dr. Roe. Sitting on the soft grass, he noticed the fresh flowers upon both graves. Tina and

Ella were beloved by everyone in Ardor Creek and Scott was used to the townspeople often replenishing the bouquets.

"I never thought I'd get to this point, Tina," he said, speaking to the headstone. "I always thought you were the only woman I'd ever fall in love with. But I think I was wrong."

Sitting back, he closed his eyes, feeling the breeze whip against his skin.

"I made so many mistakes with you," he said, lifting his lids. "I was easily forgiven because of the tragedy but you and I both know the truth. I still blame myself every day, although it's lessened over time. Dr. Roe says it will probably linger forever. Things like that often do, I guess."

Picking the grass at his side, he exhaled a breath. "I'm scared of moving on but I think I'm even more terrified I'll fuck it up again. What if I create something with her and I lose it all over again? I don't think I'd survive it. Can any person live through something like that twice?"

Silence answered him as he stared ahead, unseeing and thoughtful. After a while, he stood, caressing both the headstones before heading home. Ashlyn's kitchen was almost finished and he wanted to inspect it before they went to dinner at the pub. Attempting to shed the day's heavy reflections, he hopped in his car to head to Ashlyn's, craving her embrace and glowing smile.

On Saturday, Scott's phone lit up with a text from Ashlyn. It contained a picture of what looked to be a medical report.

Scott: Did you send me this by accident?

Ashlyn: LOL. No. It's my results from my visit to the gyno last week. All my lady parts are clean as a whistle and I have an IUD. Figured you might want to have some sexy times on the porch tonight before you tear it up next week.

Laughing, he texted back.

Scott: Sexy times without condoms?

Ashlyn: You're picking up what I'm putting down. Nice job.

Scott: I'm pretty sure I'm clean too. No one since Tina and I got tested last time I had a physical. Everything was fine.

Ashlyn: Well, then, come over at seven and let's show that porch we mean business.

Shaking his head, he could barely contain his chuckle.

Scott: Is it weird that it used to be your grandma's porch?

She shot him an eye-roll emoji.

Ashlyn: It is now. Grandma Jean was awesome but let's leave her out of this one.

Scott: Done. See you at seven.

Brimming with anticipation, Scott couldn't release his perma-grin as he drove to Ashlyn's place that evening. Hell, he didn't give a damn. The thought of making love to her skin to skin was intoxicating and he couldn't wait to connect with her that way. Once parked in her driveway, he all but ran up the stairs, smiling when she swung open the door.

"Hello, lover." Her tone was sultry and sexy as her raven black eyebrow arched above those deep green eyes. "My, you seem excited."

Encircling her wrist, he tugged her toward the porch rail, lifting her as she squealed. Setting her on the wooden surface, he devoured her lips in a searing kiss.

"Do you know how much I think about you?" he breathed into her mouth, unbuttoning her jeans as her fingers tore away his belt. "God, Ashlyn, you've consumed my soul."

She stilled, biting her lip as her eyes darted between his. "That's super romantic for a casual fling, Mr. Grillo." Her tone was teasing but he could read the sentiment in her gaze.

"There's nothing casual about my feelings for you, sweetheart," he whispered, lowering her to her feet and tugging her shirt off before crouching down. Shimmying her pants and thong down her supple legs, he pulled her sandals off and tossed her clothes aside.

Standing, he gently urged her to face the rail before unclasping her bra and throwing it on the nearby rocking chair. Splaying his hand over her upper back, he commanded softly, "Hold on tight, honey."

Ripping his shirt off, he threw it over hers before pushing his pants and boxers to his knees. Gripping her shoulder, he aligned the head of his shaft with her wet center, hissing at the intense contact.

"You ready, sweetheart?"

"Yes," she cried, knuckles white as they gripped the rail. "Fuck me hard."

Following her command, he impaled her in one thrust, groaning at the intense pleasure as her tight, wet channel choked him. Burning with arousal, he withdrew completely, loving her high-pitched whimper. Clenching his teeth, he surged back inside, her wet folds drowning him in bliss. Widening his stance, he began to fuck her in earnest, pistoning inside her drenched core over and over as she mewled beneath him.

"You're so fucking tight around my cock, honey," he growled in her ear. "I want you to come when I explode inside you." Lathering his fingers with his tongue, he reached around, finding her clit and circling it with firm, steady pressure.

"*Harder*," she demanded, causing something inside to howl as he hammered her quivering body.

"So...connected...to...you..." he managed to warble in her ear before he bit the shell. "Do you feel it, Ash?"

"Yes," she whimpered, bending farther over the balcony, her body so open it unlocked something deep within his chest. Awed by her trust, he vowed to make her scream. Intensifying the strokes of his fingers, he pounded her limp body, his brain a jumbled pile of rapidly firing nerves.

Throwing her head back, her mouth formed an 'O' before she wailed, "Coming...oh, god, coming now..."

Gritting his teeth, he buried his face in the juncture of her neck and shoulder and let everything go. All his reservations. All his fears. In that moment, there was only Ashlyn with her understanding heart and unselfish nature.

I love you...

He didn't say the words, comprehending he was nowhere near ready. There were a ton of things he needed to process before he could. But saying something didn't make it true or false, and Scott understood his feelings for Ashlyn were profound. Overcome with joy he'd found her in their huge and sometimes disconnected world, he clasped her to him as jets of release spurted into her tight warmth.

"Fuck," he growled into her neck, body jerking as it depleted. "Can't stop coming…feels too good."

Her contented sigh was melodious to his ears as she relaxed, limp and sated. "Give me all you got, buddy," she mumbled. "Here for it."

Laughter erupted in his chest as he pulsed inside her. She contracted her inner muscles, squeezing him dry, and he scraped his teeth across her skin, causing her to shiver.

They stood like that, twined together and raw as their bodies recovered. It should've been uncomfortable but, in reality, Scott had never felt so complete. Taken with the intensity of his feelings for her, he struggled to reclaim his breath.

"I take it back. Grandma Jean would be so proud right now. She was a feminist to her core and would've loved how freely we just banged on her porch. She went to Woodstock, after all. This is definitely some free love shit."

Snickering, he shook his head against her shoulder. "Thank god this place is surrounded by woods," he said, placing a kiss on her sweaty skin. "Have I told you lately how thankful I am you make me laugh?"

Wiggling into him, she threatened to set his body on fire again. Feeling his release begin to slip down their thighs, he mourned having to leave her soft grip. "A time or two."

Sliding from her, he steadied her as she turned to face him. "We're messy," she said, wrinkling her nose.

"Come on." Threading their fingers, he led her inside and up the stairs to the bathroom so they could clean up. Eventually, they recovered their strewn clothing from outside and Ashlyn threw on sweats. Scott ordered pizza and they lazed on the couch while replenishing their energy. Comfortable and quenched, they fell asleep after dinner as they watched a movie.

Around midnight, Scott awoke, emotion swishing through his frame at the sight of her body wrapped around him in the shorts and tank she'd thrown on. Careful not to wake her, he carried her upstairs, placing her on the soft sheets. After ditching his clothes, he crawled in behind her, drawing her close. She smacked her lips together before settling against him, her head on his chest and the silken skin of her thigh over his. Lost in her scent, Scott realized he felt more at home in her embrace than he did inside his own house. Too tired to grapple with the gravity of that awareness, he vowed to discuss it with Dr. Roe early next week.

As his eyes drifted shut, he listened to the steady rocking sounds above. He was used to them now and wondered if Sally Pickens was keeping watch over them. He'd never believed in ghosts but after spending so much time with Ashlyn, his mind was open to so many things it hadn't been for so very long. The pattern of the creaks was measured and always loudest when he was holding her after they made love.

"Are you trying to tell me something, Sally?" he asked softly as he stroked Ashlyn's hair. "Can you talk to them? Are they okay?"

Suddenly, the rocking noises ceased and the tiny hairs on Scott's arms prickled as he strained to hear. "Sally?"

Silence was his only response until he sighed and nestled further into Ashlyn's warmth. Holding her tight, he spoke tender words in the dark, testing them on his tongue for the day he would be ready to say them in the light.

Chapter 21

Summer rolled into fall and the last day of construction was finally on the horizon. Ashlyn stood in the front yard beside Scott, hands on her hips as she watched Dan, Larry and Caleb apply the stain to her brand new porch.

"It looks amazing. What a gorgeous entrance for everyone who takes the haunted homes tour. I'll set up my food truck in the yard on the weekends when people come through so they can have some grub along the tour. Two birds with one stone and all."

"Sounds like a great plan. Kara and Megan are excited to work the truck while you lead people through the house," Scott said, referencing the two high school students Ashlyn had hired to work weekends.

"They both seem like great young ladies. I'm stoked. The spot Chad annexed for me to park in the main square is perfect, and I'm going to try my best to sell my ass off."

Smiling, he threaded his fingers through hers. "I think you've got that covered. You're going to do great. It was so smart to get a liquor license so you can make specialty cocktails."

"Yep," she said, beaming. "The markup on alcohol is so much higher than food. And I've already got the contracts sealed with Uber Eats and Seamless so I can offer delivery."

"Holy shit, you're opening a high-end food truck." He squeezed her hand.

Biting her lip, she asked, "Am I fucking crazy?"

Facing her, he cupped her cheek with his free hand. "You're fucking beautiful," he said softly.

Those green eyes swam with emotion as Scott saw Dan approach out of the corner of his eye.

"Sorry to interrupt, boss, but Donna called me earlier and I want to make sure I tell you both before I forget."

"Forget what?" he asked.

"We're having a cookout on Saturday and want you both to come, of course. Ashlyn, you can finally meet our kids. Two of 'em are great and the other one is okay half the time."

After throwing back her head and giving a hearty laugh, she nodded. "I'd love to. I'll make something special to bring. Just have Donna let me know what she needs."

"Will do. The guys and I have really enjoyed this project, Ashlyn. We can't thank you enough for all the amazing food. I think I've gained ten pounds."

"You three were integral to me narrowing down my menu so the pleasure was all mine."

With a tilt of his head, he sauntered back toward the porch to finish the job.

"I'm going to miss them," she said, frowning. "I'll be all alone with only Sally to keep me company."

"I might stop by every now and then," Scott said, squinting as he feigned consideration.

Breathing a laugh, she gave him a soft smile. "We're getting close to having to discuss the future of this sex-only thing we've got going on."

Tightening his grip, he nodded. "I know. Maybe after the cookout on Saturday? We can talk on your beautiful new front porch."

A dark brow arched. "Is this your way of trying to goad me into christening the new porch? Because I'm open."

Leaning down, he chuckled as he kissed her. "We'll see where the day takes us. Okay, let me get to these inspections. You're distracting me, Ms. Rivers."

"By all means, Mr. Grillo."

Gesturing toward the house, she urged him to get to work.

Ashlyn had a fantastic time at Donna and Dan's cookout. Their kids, all girls aged two, four, and seven, were adorable, and she spent most of the day playing soccer with the two older girls, along with Sebastian and Charlie. Once her energy was thoroughly depleted, she headed over to grab a well-deserved beer and was taken with the toddler on Donna's lap.

"Do you want to hold her?" she asked, standing and stretching her back. "She's heavy and I need a refill."

"Sure," Ashlyn said, extending her arms. "Hey, Mary, do you want to sit on my lap for a little while?"

The girl looked at her mom, chewing on her tiny finger before Donna nodded. "That's Ashlyn, honey. She's really nice. I bet she'd draw on the sidewalk with you."

"I love sidewalk chalk," Ashlyn said, sitting down on the concrete and reaching for an orange stick. "I can draw the sun with this one." Placing the tip against the surface, she drew a circle.

Mary trailed over on her chubby legs, plopping down and picking a blue stick from the bucket before proceeding to destroy the perfect circle Ashlyn had drawn. "Wow, Mary, you're really good."

"Sunshine," was her excited reply through small, gapped teeth.

"Sunshine is right, sister. Let's draw more." As she played with the little girl, something welled in her gut, growing like a seed that had been planted long ago but had only recently been watered. Reveling in Mary's smiles and laughter, Ashlyn let the feeling take hold. She and Robert had always discussed having children after they were married, but it had always seemed so far away. But she was in her thirties now and it made sense the longing would amplify as she got older.

Glancing at Scott, she noticed him watching her, a strange look on his face as Peter droned on about baseball beside him. Did he want more children after what had happened to Ella? It was something they'd never discussed. Adding it to the tally of things she was determined to discuss this evening, she steeled herself for a frank, honest conversation. Anxiety began to sprout in her belly and she tamped it down, reminding herself it was better to be up front than push things aside. She would never make that mistake again.

The drive to her house was quiet as she sat beside Scott, absently staring at those broad hands upon the wheel. Would she feel them again after tonight or were their visions of the future too different? Sadness ripped through her at the possibility of ending their romantic relationship but she was a different person than she'd been with Robert. She wouldn't remain in a situation she knew wouldn't be fruitful for her future. She owed it to herself to want more. To *choose* more.

Since the night was balmy, they decided to hang on the porch, and Ashlyn made coffee for Scott before pouring herself some wine. Handing him the steaming cup, she sat beside him in the rocking chair as the crickets sang under the stars.

"That was fun today," he said, sipping the coffee.

"Sure was. Donna and Dan's kids are adorable. I think I fell in love with Mary."

"I think the feeling was mutual. She seemed enamored with you."

Sipping her wine, she swallowed before leaning her head back on the wood. "I want them, Scott. At least two, maybe three. In all their dirty-diapered glory and temper tantrums, I want them with every part of my soul."

Expelling a slow breath, he set the cup in the saucer before placing it on the little table beside the chair. Crossing his hands over his abdomen, he rocked. "Having kids is awesome. I miss Ella so much."

Stopping the tears from forming was as futile as turning the sky purple, so she just let them be. They trailed down her cheeks as she observed the sorrow on his handsome face. "I wish I knew how to bring her back. How to help you heal. How to love you enough that you never hurt again."

Reaching over, he grabbed her hand. "You've done so much, honey. You know that, right?"

Feeling her eyes dart between his, she softly asked, "But?"

Sighing, he disengaged his hand before running it through his hair. Standing, he trailed to the railing and rested his palms flat, staring out over the grass. Ashlyn let him stew, knowing he had to process the conversation in his own way.

"At this point, not moving forward into something more serious has nothing to do with you." Turning, he leaned against the rail, crossing his arms and ankles as they stretched in front of his body. "Nor does it have anything to do with my feelings for you. They're real, Ash. More real than I ever could've imagined when you came barreling into my life and almost murdered me atop a ladder."

Breathing a laugh, she wiped away the tears. "Yeah, attempted homicide wasn't exactly what I was going for."

His eyes were tender as his lips curved in the moonlight. "You were so fierce. So beautiful. I think I knew from that moment you'd change my life."

The words laced through every cell in her heart, constricting the organ as it pounded in her chest. "But you have reservations?"

Inhaling, his nostrils slightly flared as he stared absently toward the ground. "Remember when I said life gets in the way of me keeping in touch with Tina's mom?"

Nodding, Ashlyn felt her eyebrows draw together at his solemn tone.

"Well, the story's a bit more complicated. Only Peter and Carrie know the truth."

"What's the truth?"

Pursing his lips, he contemplated his words. "Tina and I had a rough time after Ella was born. She experienced postpartum depression and we were exhausted from being new parents. The first year was really tough but we were on our way to piecing back together our marriage."

"That must've been really hard."

"It was," he said with a tilt of his head. "We'd lost the easy flow of our relationship and ended up fighting a lot more after Ella was born. Things got better as she grew closer to turning two but we still had some epic blowouts."

"I'm no expert but marriage is tough. The divorce rate certainly proves that."

Nodding, he continued. "We always loved each other. I never doubted that. But our fights were terrible and something I deeply regret. Two nights before the accident, we got into a terrible argument."

Dread filled Ashlyn as she anticipated where the story was headed.

"She accused me of being emotionally unavailable and I told her to take Ella and stay with her mom for a few days if being in my presence was so terrible. And, well…she did."

Setting the forgotten wine on the porch, Ashlyn stood and went to him, palming his face as the tears began anew. "Oh, Scott."

"Yeah," he said, sniffling. "That was the last time I saw them. She stayed for two days and we spoke on the phone a few times, although the anger was still there. I told her we'd work everything out when she got home."

Desperate to comfort him as pain clenched her heart, she slid her arms around his waist and squeezed for dear life. His arms surrounded her, taking solace as he rubbed his cheek over her hair.

"Well, you can see why Tina's mom never forgave me. I think she always blamed me for putting them in the position where they would encounter the drunk driver."

Drawing back, she shook her head. "You can't know that. There are a million scenarios where bad things happen. Please don't tell me you blame yourself."

"I did, for a while, until the therapy kicked in." Stroking the hair at her temple, his eyes glistened from his own tears. "But worse was the reaction from everyone in town. They all treated me like some saint or hero or martyr or…well, whatever it was, it was better than what I deserved."

"No, it wasn't," Ashlyn said, tightening her hand on his cheek. "You experienced a devastating loss, Scott. I'm so glad you had a support network to lift you up."

He remained silent, his fingers soft over her hair. They stayed like that for a while, allowing the moment to settle in. Eventually, she slid her thumb over his bottom lip. "You're afraid to experience happiness again."

"Terrified," he said, shoulders lifting in a slight shrug. "I think the fear that I could lose people I love that deeply again is stronger than the desire to experience the love. I've talked about it for years with my therapist."

"What does she say about it?"

"She says Tina and Ella would want me to be happy."

"Do you believe that?"

His breath was shallow as he pondered. "Sometimes."

Feeling her lips curve, she lifted her shoulder. "Well, that's better than never."

Chuckling, he nodded. "Yeah." Stroking her temple, he looked so sad. "I'm so sorry you have to deal with this baggage. You probably should've dated Chad when you first got here. He's a lot more fun and laid back."

"Eh, turns out I kinda have a thing for grumpy, sexy contractors, baggage or not."

Gently, Ashlyn extricated from his embrace, needing to be on solid ground as she spoke. "First of all, thank you for telling me this. It's extremely meaningful that you trust me enough to confide this in me, Scott."

"Thank you for listening."

Sliding her hands in the back pockets of her jeans, she formulated her thoughts. "I'm so happy you loved Tina and Ella so much. It's amazing for this unlucky-in-love city girl who still holds out hope of finding the love of her life one day."

His throat bobbed as he stared back, silent.

"But if I'm not careful, you're going to become the man I fall head over heels in love with." When he opened his mouth to speak, she held up a hand. "Please. Let me just say this while it's fresh in my mind."

"Okay."

Inhaling, she struggled to get the words right. "I don't want to push you into something you're not ready for or offer ultimatums. Love doesn't work that way. It's one of my biggest lessons from my previous relationship. But I also want to be with someone who loves me with their whole heart. Who truly believes I'm their soulmate. Maybe that's naive, but it's what I want and I'm not sure I even realized it until Robert cheated on me. He ended up giving me the gift of starting over and finding someone who would truly make me happy. Someone with whom I can build a family and grow old with."

"You deserve that, Ashlyn."

"I know," she said softly. "I believe that with all my heart. You've already had a family and a soulmate so I can accept those things might not be a priority for you. But I can't push away what I want anymore. I did that for so long and wasted so many years. I won't do it again, Scott."

Blowing a breath through puffed cheeks, he lifted his hand. "So where do we go from here?"

Heart splintering in her chest, Ashlyn spoke the words that were so painful but she knew in her soul were right. "We need to take a break. Take some time to think about what we truly want. You need to decide if you're willing to take a chance on having a family again, even if it's terrifying. I need to figure out if I'm okay with being the person you're with because your family was ripped away from you."

"No," he said, stepping forward to take her face in his hands. "You're not some consolation prize, Ashlyn. Whatever happens, I need you to know that. You're the person who's pieced together so many fragments I didn't realize were broken."

"Yes, but maybe I'm meant to be with someone who wasn't shattered in the first place."

Anger flashed in his eyes and she shook her head. "That came out wrong." Rubbing her forehead, frustration began to simmer. "I just...I'll always be your second, Scott, if we decide to really go for this. Your second wife. The mother of your second child. It's...well, it's a *lot*. You get that, right?"

Dropping his hands, he stepped back. "I get that it hurts to be accused of making someone second best when that's not at all how I feel."

Tamping down her anger, she straightened her spine. "I'm not accusing you. I just wonder if you can give me what I want."

Judging by the firm line of his lips and the muscle twitching in his jaw, Ashlyn could tell he was furious. And hurt. Fuck, she'd hurt him, although she hadn't meant to. "I'm really screwing this up."

"Yeah, you really are."

Realizing her patience was wearing thin, she tamped down the urge to scream. "I don't want to argue with you. We always knew this conversation would be hard. We need to take some time apart to grapple with the repercussions."

"That's the difference here, Ashlyn. I have no desire to spend time apart from you."

"So, what?" she asked, exasperated. "We'll just fuck around and stay in our serious/non-serious relationship forever? I don't want that, Scott."

"You were fine with it when we first went down this road."

"That was before I fell in love with you!" she screamed, fury now bubbling inside her veins. "There, is that what you want to hear? Because I'm pretty damn sure you're not going to say it back."

Heavy breaths exited his lungs as he stared at her. "Ashlyn..."

"Nope, not quite what I was looking for there, buddy. Nice try, though."

"You always knew—"

"Yes, I knew. Just like I know I'm not doing this anymore." Picking up her glass, she stomped toward the front door. "I don't want us to say harsh things to each other, Scott. We're better than that. Take some time to really think. You deserve that and I don't begrudge you for it. I'll wait as long as I can. If you don't figure it out before I'm ready to move on, then hopefully we can still be friends. I truly want that because my life would suck without you in it, whatever form our relationship takes." Giving him a nod, she stepped inside. "You have my number."

Closing the door, she set the glass on the nearby table before leaning back against it. Sounds muffled on the porch before she heard his car engine and the subsequent sound of gravel under the tires as he drove away. Sliding down the wooden door, she buried her face in her upturned knees and allowed herself to cry.

After a restless night, Ashlyn rubbed her swollen eyes and lifted her phone from the bedside table. Opening her camera app, she turned the lens on herself, noting her puffy face and bloodshot eyes. It was early and she'd planned to run with the group today but realized the chances of that happening were slim to none. Instead, she debated whether she wanted to bury herself in a vat of rocky road or order an extra-large pizza and overload on comfort carbs. Both options sounded fantastic, honestly. Yep, she was going to do both.

The phone rang, jarring her as she stared at the incoming caller ID. Scott was video calling her. Deciding not to be a coward, she answered.

"If you're calling to cement your decision to never see me again, this is great timing. I look like shit."

His smile was sad as he stared at her with his own reddened eyes. "I'm not a bastion of sexiness right now either."

"Eh, you're okay," she said softly. Sighing, she shook her head on the pillow. "I'm so sorry, Scott."

"I called to apologize to you, Ash, not the other way around. I realized when I left that I handled the whole thing terribly. I should've learned by now that nothing good comes from walking away when you're angry."

"We're only human," she said, turning to her side and almost cuddling the phone like a lovelorn sap. "All we can do is be honest with each other and try our best."

Glancing down, he contemplated before speaking. "Your words meant so much to me, Ashlyn," he said, reclaiming her gaze. "That's the most important thing I need you to know."

"They're true," she said, lifting a shoulder. "But love is only the beginning. Building a life together requires so much more. That's why I suggested we both take some time to really think about things."

"You were right." His grin was adorable as he gazed at her. "How in the hell are you so smart?"

"It's a burden but I carry on," she teased.

He was quiet for a moment. "My feelings for you aren't in question, although I'm certainly not going to dive into them on the phone. What I question is if I'm ready to take the leap again. I just don't know if I am, Ash."

"I understand." Tears welled as she strove to push them away. "It's a really important decision, Scott. I don't mind giving you time."

"It's not fair to ask you to wait for me to get my shit together."

"You didn't ask. I'm over here making my own decisions. If Jason Momoa comes to town and you still haven't figured it out, I'm definitely choosing him. So, you'd better get to thinking, buddy."

Laughing, he nodded. "I don't stand a chance against Jason Momoa."

Winking, she said, "I like your odds."

"Okay," he said, exhaling. "I'm going to process this and discuss it with Dr. Roe. I don't know how long it will take. I wish I could give you some sort of timeframe."

"That's okay. You have my number. And I'll see you when we jog."

"You know I hate jogging with other people. I put up with it because I get to spend time with you. I miss our one on one sessions."

"Well, we'll go jogging alone, just the two of us, one day soon," she said, wondering deep in her heart if it would happen. There was a very real possibility her window of spending one on one time with Scott had closed. Only time would tell.

"I'd like that. I was so bummed to wake up without you beside me, honey."

"Me too."

Huffing a breath, he ran a hand through his hair. "Okay. I've got work to do. Don't be a stranger, okay?"

"Okay," she whispered.

"Ash?"

"Yeah?"

"Remember I need the push. It probably isn't fair to ask that of you but don't forget."

"I won't."

"Have a good day, honey."

"You too."

Clicking off the phone, she tossed it on the nightstand and groaned. Sitting up, she rubbed her eyes and gave herself a pep talk. "No moping, Rivers. You have a crap ton of things to do in this new life and it's time you get to it." Tossing off the covers, she squared her shoulders and began the day.

Chapter 22

Scott threw himself into work, focusing on his ongoing projects and preparing for the Kingsley job in early spring. Several sites needed to wrap up construction before winter arrived and it required intense focus as September turned into October. The breakneck schedule wasn't conducive to the intense amount of reflection he needed to do about the situation with Ashlyn, which Dr. Roe pointed out in one of their early-October sessions.

"What are you hoping will happen, Scott?" she'd asked in her always firm but compassionate tone. "That you'll procrastinate long enough she ends up making the decision it won't work? Are you trying to avoid that responsibility?"

"Maybe," he said, fingers twining in his lap. "If she decides I'm not worth it then I can tell myself it was the best thing for her. That I'm doing her a favor by letting her find someone who isn't broken inside."

"And you'll still be the good guy because she ended things. The saint of Ardor Creek."

Grimacing, he ran his hand over his face. "I hate that stupid nickname. I certainly don't deserve it."

"Why are you reverting to blaming yourself? I thought you let go of that."

Sighing, he shrugged. "What if it happens again, Doc? What if she heads to the city to see a friend and never comes home? What if we have kids and something happens to one of them? How can a person live through something like that twice?"

"Humans are resilient," Dr. Roe said, smiling. "You pick up the pieces and try your best to make it through another day, even with all the pain. The burden is certainly lessened if you have a strong, loving partner to support you."

"She says she'll always be second. I hate that she feels that way but I don't know how to reconcile loving Tina and loving her. Is it disingenuous to what I had with my wife to love Ashlyn?"

"No," she said, shaking her head. "Love is the most amazing emotion we have, Scott. You're extremely lucky to have found it with two women who love you back. It would be a shame to squander it this second time around."

Tears stung his eyes. "How can I have another child...another little girl...and not think of Ella?"

"Why wouldn't you want to think of her? You should celebrate her and tell any children you have about their sister. Do you think Ashlyn would be open to that? To talking about Tina and Ella with the children you would have together?"

"Yes," he said, without any doubt. "She's amazing. Sometimes I wonder how she's so emotionally stable. It's disconcerting."

"Well, from what you've told me, it sounds like she wasn't always that way. She experienced painful lessons and learned from her mistakes. That's what one must do if they want to see positive change. I think witnessing her strength is good for you."

"She's unbelievable. I mean, she picked up and moved to a new town, started a business, charmed everyone in Ardor Creek. I honestly think she might be too good for me."

"Well, don't tell her that," she teased. "Seems she hasn't figured it out."

Breathing a laugh, he pondered. "What if she does? What if the marriage devolves like it did with Tina? I mean, we were getting back on track and I think we would've figured things out but I'll never really know."

"There's no crystal ball with relationships, Scott. You have to throw your hat in the ring, do the best you can and see what happens. That's all any of us can hope for."

"You're right. I guess I'm just really risk-averse."

"That makes sense but it leads to a very lonely and unfulfilling life in most circumstances."

"True," he said, rubbing his forehead in frustration. "I miss holding Ashlyn so much."

"Enough to give her what she wants?"

Gazing at his lap, he struggled to answer. "I don't know."

When the session was over, Scott couldn't shake the nerves the intense conversation had spurred. Calling Peter over his Bluetooth, he asked if he wanted to get a drink at the pub.

"You mean two iced teas for our sad souls?" his friend teased. "It's karaoke night. Are you sure you're up for that?"

"I'm definitely not singing but I don't want to go home. It's too quiet there."

"Well, it will certainly be loud at the pub. I'll see you there."

An hour later, they were seated at the bar when Ashlyn walked in with Carrie.

"Hi, guys," she said, her smile gorgeous under those eyes he longed for every night in his cold bed. Eyes that had stared into his soul as he'd finally found a connection he was convinced he'd never find again.

"Hey," he said, unable to contain his grin. "You two here for karaoke?"

"Yep," Carrie said. "Chad's coming too. He wants to buy Ashlyn some drinks for her grand opening on Monday."

"I should be buying him drinks since he fast-tracked the permits for me, but I'll take it," Ashlyn said.

Warning bells sounded in Scott's brain at the thought of another man buying Ashlyn drinks. A man who was handsome, charming, and didn't have a shit ton of baggage on his shoulders. "Is he bringing Charity?"

"They broke up," Carrie said. "Another on Chad's 'love 'em and leave 'em' list. She'll do fine though. She was a great girl and I'll miss seeing her around. She wasn't a local like we are," she whispered conspiratorially to Ashlyn.

"Am I a local now?" she asked, flashing a smile.

"You sure are, honey," Carrie said, placing her arm over her shoulders. "Come on. Let's get the front table. Have fun, boys.

Peter, you're singing Atlantic Starr with me before the night is over."

"You got it, Care Bear," he said with a wink.

They strolled away and Chad breezed in a few minutes later, looking as ruggedly handsome as a damn movie star. Flooded with jealousy, which he knew was ridiculous, Scott waved to Terry. "Give me something with vodka in it for the next round."

Her brows lifted behind the bar. "You sure about that?"

"Yep. I haven't had a real drink in years. Figure it's time."

"You really want to do this, Scott?" Peter asked.

Nodding, he looked at Terry. "Whatever you like. Bartender's choice." She returned a few minutes later with a vodka soda, splash of Sprite, and cranberry. "Here you go. Keep an eye on him," she said to Peter.

Scott grimaced at the first sip, the taste bitter on his tongue.

"Did we really drink vodka straight from the bottle in high school?"

"Yep," Peter said, patting him on the back. "Pretty gross."

"Disgusting." Although the drink was terrible, Scott forced it down as he observed Ashlyn sing with Carrie. A few songs later, Chad joined Ashlyn on stage and they sang a duet together as they gazed into each other's eyes. Wanting to pound the bar in, Scott ordered another vodka soda.

"Hey, man," Peter said, concerned. "Go easy. You're just getting back on the horse."

"I'm fine," he muttered, feeling the liquor course through his veins as intoxication set in. "I've been a saint for so long. I get to make mistakes sometimes too."

"Oh, brother," Peter murmured. "I don't like where this is going."

After an hour and two more drinks, Scott was officially plowed. Swiveling around in the bar seat, he observed Ashlyn's upturned face as she sat beside Chad, his arm over her shoulders and not an inch between them. Furious, he stood and began to walk toward them before Peter grabbed his wrist. "Not a good idea, man."

Shaking him off, Scott stalked over, wondering why his head felt disconnected from his body and his legs weighed a hundred pounds. Man, he hadn't been drunk in so long he'd forgotten how it felt.

"He's dated every woman in town, Ashlyn," Scott said in a nasty tone. "If you're trying to make me jealous, you should do it with someone else."

Slowly turning her head, she glared at him, anger marring her expression. "*Excuse me*?"

Chad stood, nostrils flaring as a muscle clenched in his jaw. "We've been friends a long time, Scott, but there's a line. Go home. You're drunk and you're acting like an ass."

"She loves *me*," he said, feeling like the world was crumbling around him. "You're wasting your time."

"Okay, that's enough." Standing, Ashlyn faced him, full of wrath. "I've been more than understanding but you do *not* get to come in here and throw around things we discussed in private. We are *not* together and you have no claim over me, Scott. If I want to hang out with Chad or anyone else, that's none of your damn business."

"Like hell, it isn't!" Jabbing his finger in her face, he was overcome with the need to hurt her even half as much as he was hurting. "You said you would give me time to process."

"And I am," she said, batting his hand away. "In the meantime, I'm hanging out with Chad and Carrie. If you can't handle that, *you're* the one with the problem."

"Come on, buddy," Peter said, grabbing his arm. "Let's get you home."

"You said you loved me," he all but pleaded, craving the words. Needing her so desperately he ached with yearning.

Disappointment swam in her eyes as she stared into his soul. "Go home, Scott."

Something tugged at his arm and he followed the sensation, realizing moments later he was stuffed into Peter's front seat.

"She said she loved me, Peter," he mumbled, cradling his forehead in his palm.

"Yes, I know. And now, the entire bar knows, which means the whole town will know tomorrow. Way to go, man. Good grief."

"Why would she say it if she didn't mean it?" he asked, relaxing into the seat as Peter drove.

"She wouldn't. The question is, why didn't you say it back?"

Wanting to melt into a pile of despair, he shook his head. "Because it hurts and I'm so scared. Loving someone hurts, Peter."

"I know that's what love felt like to you for a long time, Scott, but I promise that's not true. It's time you let yourself experience the good parts of love. The happy parts."

"I want to be happy," he murmured, feeling his eyelids droop. "I wish I knew how."

"I know, man," his friend said, his tone sad. "I know."

When they arrived at his house, Peter slung Scott's arm over his shoulder, helping him climb the stairs before he fell to the bed. Opening his eyes, he saw his friend place a cup of water and a bottle of ibuprofen on the nightstand.

"You're going to feel like shit tomorrow. Pop two of these before you pass out." He shook the pill bottle. Giving a nod, Peter retreated, flipping off the light as he exited the bedroom.

Scott downed two pills and collapsed on the bed, face smushed against the pillow. It wasn't nearly as rewarding as holding Ashlyn but he figured he didn't really deserve that honor anymore. Understanding he'd have a lot to answer for when he awoke, he closed his eyes and passed out.

Chapter 23

Thursday morning arrived with a hangover so intense, Scott wondered if the universe was trying to rip out his intestines. After several instances of hugging his toilet, he finally found the energy to dress and head into the office. As the bell sounded above his head, he encountered Carrie's annoyed gaze as she sat behind her desk.

"Your messages are on your desk," she said, chin held high as she resumed typing.

"Okay," he sighed, setting his briefcase on the counter. "Go ahead and give it to me."

Arching a brow, she asked, "Are you ready? Because I'm not going to go easy on you."

The corner of his lips curved. "Ready."

Standing, she placed her hands on her hips. "First of all, you were a huge dick to Chad, who is one of your oldest and closest friends. That right there is completely unacceptable. But the way you spoke to Ashlyn? Tossing around words you spoke in private that were meaningful and only meant for you two? How could you, Scott?"

Blowing out a breath, he shook his head. "It's unforgivable. I feel terrible. I don't know what to say. I'm an ass."

"You certainly are. You hurt her terribly. Is that what you wanted? The Scott I know doesn't go around hurting people, especially people as amazing as Ashlyn."

"I think I want to sabotage it," he said softly, rubbing his forehead. "If I mess it up and make her hate me, I don't have to try again. I won't have to lose anyone again. I'm so afraid of losing them all over again, Carrie."

Her features softened before she approached. Sliding her arms around his waist, she squeezed. "I know it's terrifying. But I think you already love her, Scott."

Staring into her green eyes, he nodded. "I do."

Her resulting smile was brilliant. "Wow. That's awesome. You need to tell her."

"If I tell her, she's going to want more."

"Then you need to give her more."

Cupping her cheek, he grinned. "Is it that easy?"

Nodding, she bit her lip. "When you realize you love someone, I think it is. Easy and hard, all at once."

"I've been making it really hard, Carrie."

"Well, you're a man," she teased, stepping out of his embrace. "You all are idiots most of the time."

Chuckling, he asked, "Does that include Peter?"

Scoffing, she rolled her eyes. "That definitely includes Peter."

His eyes darted between hers, dying to ask so many questions.

"I still love him, Scott. I'll always love him."

"Then why—?"

Holding up a hand, she cut him off. "It's never really been our time and I've pretty much given up hope we'll grow into each other one day. But you and Ashlyn? It's your time, Scott." Stepping forward, she lifted to her toes and kissed him softly on the cheek, wiping away the gloss with her thumb. "Seize it while you can. It's so precious. You know that better than anyone."

"Thank you, Carrie," he whispered.

Nodding, she gave him a glowing smile. "Go love her back, Scott. I can't wait to see what you two build together."

Heeding his dear friend's words, Scott steeled himself to walk down the long, winding, and scary path of embracing love again.

By the time Sunday arrived, Scott was pretty sure this new path he was on was a complete waste of time. Mostly because the woman he'd finally decided he couldn't live without was avoiding him like the plague. He'd called and texted her several times, all with no response, and when he'd shown up to run with the group on Friday morning, she was a no-show. On Saturday, he thought about showing up at her house but figured that might be construed as borderline stalking, so he sent her a bouquet of flowers instead with a note he hoped would make her chuckle.

I'm so sorry, Ash. Please let me make it up to you. I miss you with all my heart.

Love, Your Grumpy Contractor

Unfortunately, it must not have been as witty as he thought because all he got in response were crickets.

On Sunday, he awoke with a palpable desire to visit Tina and Ella. Throwing on his coat to ward off the October breeze, he headed to the cemetery. As he approached their graves, he stopped short as shock pervaded his veins. Ashlyn stood above the graves, placing a bundle of flowers over each one. Unsure what to do, he tentatively advanced.

"Hey," she said, not making eye contact as she arranged the flowers to sit against one of the headstones. "Thought I might see you here."

"Hey," he said, thrusting his hands in his pockets so he didn't reach for her since he was desperate to touch her. "Nice flowers."

Tossing him a look, she arched her brows. "Well, some jerk sent them to me and I figured I could rearrange them and put them to good use. I usually bring carnations but the different colored roses are a nice touch."

Realization swamped him. "How long have you been coming here?"

Squinting, she contemplated. "Since June, I think? It was nice to visit and bring fresh flowers. I like to sit and talk to them, which would probably be weird if you didn't already know I believe in ghosts. I talk to Sally and Grandma Jean so why not Tina and Ella?

They were really important to you and that made them important to me. Also, I was really curious. Sitting here with them brought me peace." Her forehead creased. "Okay, you're looking at me like I'm nuts."

Awed by her, he took a step closer. "I don't think you're nuts." Cupping her face, he shook his head. "I think you're amazing."

Her smile clicked so many pieces of his heart into place, he felt it shift in his chest.

"I'm so sorry, Ashlyn."

"I know," she said, placing her palm over his pec. "And we need to have that discussion but not here. How about sometime this week."

"I'd say I'll text you but I think you blocked me."

Laughing, she bit her lip. "I didn't block you. I was just ignoring you. I'm allowed to do that, Scott, especially since you were a huge dick on Wednesday night."

"I was," he said, overcome with joy that he was holding her again. "Do you think you can forgive me?"

Her features scrunched. "Maybe. Groveling is good and possibly a killer foot massage. Let's start there and I'll reassess."

Chuckling, he rested his forehead against hers. "I have no problem with groveling."

Rising to her toes, she gave him a sweet kiss. "Text me tomorrow." Stepping from his embrace, she said, "Have a good visit." Giving a wave, she left him on the soft grass, marveling at her magnificence.

Lowering to the ground, he faced the headstones. "I love her, guys. I really hope you're okay with that because I've finally reached the point where the love outweighs the fear." Closing his eyes, he tilted his face to the sky, searching for confirmation.

As the soft breeze caressed his face, Scott released every last ounce of hesitation to the wind, letting it carry the doubt away and leaving optimistic anticipation in its wake.

Monday arrived, packaged with the terrible energy one observed when two freight trains collided. That was what Ashlyn equated it to as she stared at her phone in disbelief. Earlier that month, she'd set up profiles for her food truck on Yelp, Open Table, and other sites, understanding that great reviews led to more customers. When she opened the apps on Monday morning, however, she was in for a rude awakening.

Her food truck, which she'd lovingly named "Grandma Jean's Gourmet", had over one hundred one-star reviews on all the sites she'd so meticulously set up over the previous weeks. Not understanding how a business that wasn't open yet could have so many bad reviews, she began scouring them as realization dawned. The most liked review was from an account named "RT". Robert Torre. Understanding her ex had created a plethora of fake accounts from which to malign her business with bad reviews, Ashlyn almost smashed her phone into the wall. Furious, she called Carrie.

"Oh, sweetie, that's terrible," her friend said. "I'm so sorry. What can I do to help?"

"You guys know a local lawyer, right? I want to check my options and see how I can get the fake reviews removed. I'm going to email the review sites but the likelihood of getting them to remove reviews without professional help isn't great."

"Yes, I'm going to call Mark Lancaster for you and update him before asking him to give you a call. He's our local attorney and smart as hell. I'll make sure he knows you're a local so he gives this priority."

"Thank you, Carrie," she said, overwhelmed at the gravity of the task before her. "Having so many bad reviews is terrible. No one is going to want to come within a hundred feet of me. Half of them said the food made them barf. God, Robert is such an asshole! I swear, I'm going to murder him."

"Screw that bastard. We won't let him win. Everyone in this town has your back, honey. We take care of our own. Got it?"

"I'm so thankful for you, Carrie," she said, clutching the phone. "You're such a good friend."

"Let me call Mark. I'll be in touch."

Clicking off the phone, Ashlyn prepared for her first day, wondering if she was already doomed. After driving the truck into town, she parked on the agreed-upon corner she'd discussed with Chad when securing the permits. She'd prepared a lot of food in anticipation of being busy for her opening day. Unfortunately, her first day was a dud and she barely cleared a hundred dollars. Discouraged, she packed up around eight p.m. and drove home, wanting to put the terrible day behind her.

When the phone rang, she answered as she sat on the couch, defeated.

"Did it get any better after I stopped by this afternoon?" Scott asked, concern lacing his tone.

"Nope. I'm ruined. Who wants to eat at a food truck where all the reviews say the food makes them puke? I heard back from two of the sites today who say they won't remove the reviews without litigation. This is going to cost me so much money. I can't believe Robert is this vindictive. I'm so discouraged, Scott." Feeling the tears run down her cheeks, she wiped them away, furious and frustrated.

"I can be there in five minutes if you want, honey."

Sighing, she contemplated the repercussions of relying on him before they'd worked out all their other issues. Deciding it wouldn't be smart, she declined his offer.

"I want to support you," he said, his tone sincere. "You've been so supportive of me. Please let me be there for you."

"That's what partners do, Scott, and you're not my partner yet. I don't want to depend on you when there's so much still undefined between us. I'm tough and think I just need to get some sleep."

"We need to find time to talk, Ash. There are so many things I want to say. That I'm finally ready to say."

"I wish I was in the headspace to hear it, but I'm just not right now. I need you to respect that."

"Okay." His concern filtered through the phone, almost tangible. "Please call me whenever you feel like talking. Even if it's three in the morning."

Feeling her lips twitch, she said, "That's usually when I talk to Sally. You'll have to wait in line."

His deep chuckle surrounded her, enveloping her in its warmth. “I would never mess with Sally Pickens. She’s a tough one.”

“She is. Good night, Scott. Thanks for checking on me.”

“Always, sweetheart. Talk soon.”

Ending the call, Ashlyn rested her head on the couch, wondering how in the hell she was going to clean up the mess that now comprised her life.

Chapter 24

By the time Friday arrived, Ashlyn was ready to pack it all up, move to Alaska and never enter the continental forty-eight again. A person could hide forever in the Alaskan wilderness, right? It would save her from having to admit she was a huge, glaring failure. The reviews had all but ruined her and she'd barely had any customers all week.

Sighing, she glanced at her watch before staring back at Main Street. The town was decorated for that weekend's Halloween parade and she was excited to lead the haunted homes tour through her house. At least *that* wasn't a disaster. She planned to remain open on Main Street until five o'clock before driving the truck to her home. The first tour group would come through at seven, with two more following at eight and nine o'clock. The town trolleybuses drove people to the various homes and cemeteries on the tour, and Ashlyn hoped people would be hungry. Perhaps they'd try her food while they stopped at her home since there was no other option.

"You're really shooting for the bottom of the barrel, Rivers," she muttered. "Hoping people buy your food as an alternative to starvation. Yikes."

Squinting in the late October sun, she saw Scott exit GDC and wave to a van that pulled up along the sidewalk. Pointing to her truck, he seemed to be directing them to drive toward her. It was almost noon so perhaps he was trying to get them to try Grandma Jean's Gourmet for lunch. She appreciated the sentiment, especially since she'd barely spoken to him all week. Things had been so intense during the opening and prepping for the haunted homes tour, she just hadn't been able to deal with her complex feelings for Scott as well.

Several people exited the businesses along Main Street and began to walk to her truck, parked near the large clock at the head of the square. The van drove slowly toward her, parking nearby so she could see the side which read, **Channel 4 News, Scranton**. Confused, she exited the truck and stepped onto the street.

"Hey, Ash," Scott said, approaching her. "You ready?"

"Ready for what?" she asked, gesturing to the news van. "Did I miss a big Ardor Creek breaking news story?"

"You sure did," he said, grinning. "We're going to make Grandma Jean's Gourmet go viral."

A team of people exited the van, and an attractive young man approached, hand extended. "I'm Gus Rosendale, Ms. Rivers," he said, shaking her hand. "The local restaurant reporter. We're excited to do a feature on your food truck. Everyone here has signed waivers to let us film them eating your food, and we'll get some interviews too. Then, we'll interview you. Sound good?"

Overcome with elation, she smiled up at Scott. "Did you put this together?"

"You've worked so hard, Ash," he said, tucking a strand of hair behind her ear. "I'm not going to let that asshole ruin it. The whole town is ready to support you."

"I'm ready for that brisket sandwich," Carrie said, coming to stand beside Scott. "Can't wait to try it."

"And I'm going to try the carnitas tacos," Peter said before Chad chimed in beside him.

"I hear you have food truck garlic fries?" the mayor asked. "Yes, please," he said, lifting a finger.

Feeling her chin quiver, Ashlyn stared at them through glassy eyes. "You guys are awesome."

"We'd like to get shots of you preparing the food too, Ms. Rivers," the reporter said. "It will only take a few minutes for us to set up."

"That's perfect," she said, excitement thrumming through her whole body. "I'm ready. Let's to it." Hopping back into the truck, she got to work.

An hour later, the reporter and his team had gotten so much footage, Ashlyn was sure she had enough to splice into posts on her social media sites for months. So thankful to Scott—and to everyone in Ardor Creek—she stepped outside the truck to do one last interview with Gus. The cameraman trained the camera on her and Gus held the microphone, asking her some final questions. Scott appeared out of the corner of her eye and walked into the shot as they were filming.

"Um, should we cut?" she asked, wondering why he had a weird smile pasted on his handsome face.

"No, ma'am," Gus said, "we're finally getting to the good part. Scott, whenever you're ready."

Eyebrows drawing together, she faced the man who'd stolen her heart, feeling her knees shake as he lowered to one knee.

"Scott?" she whispered. "What are you doing?"

"Since I made an ass of myself, I wanted to tell you I was sorry for announcing our private conversation to the entire town," he said, clutching her hand in both of his. "That was really awful of me, Ashlyn, and I hope you can forgive me."

"I forgive you," she said, cupping his jaw. "And besides, it was true. I do love you, Scott."

He closed his eyes for a moment before opening them to stare up at her, the orbs clear and blazing with emotion. "I love you too, Ashlyn. With my entire soul. I figured I needed to put us on even ground and announce it to the world." Tilting his head toward the camera crew, he said, "Well, to all of Central Pennsylvania, at least."

Laughing, Ashlyn bit her lip. "Talk about a viral moment."

Gazing up at her, he squeezed her hand. "I want to build a future with you if you'll have me, honey. I'm still afraid of so much but I'm even more terrified of living one more day without you as my partner. The first step is letting me move in with you if you'll consider that."

"What about your house?"

"I put it on the market yesterday," he said, shrugging. "I love that house but it was built for my past. I'm ready to live in a place that represents my future. I heard your contractor did pretty great work and would love to see it in action." He gave her a wink.

A tear ran down her cheek as she breathed a laugh. "Only if Sally says it's okay."

Nodding, he said, "We'll ask her tonight."

Caressing his jaw, she said in an aching voice, "I'd love for you to move in with me, Scott."

Rising, he lifted her in his arms, twirling her around as she held on for dear life. Coming to a halt, he set her on her feet and rested his forehead against hers. "I love you so much, Ashlyn. I want to give you everything you've ever dreamed of. I'm ready to be your soulmate."

Lifting to her toes, she kissed him through the tears, joy encompassing every cell in her body. "I'm so proud of you for choosing to move forward, Scott, and I'm so excited to build something with you."

"There's so much more, honey, I promise," he murmured against her lips. "One step at a time. Thank god you're so patient with me. I almost blew it. Man, I'm an idiot."

"Hey, you're my idiot," she teased, giving him one last kiss before the crowd erupted into cheers around them.

"Well, I think we've got it," Gus said to his team. "Thanks for letting us interview you today, Ms. Rivers."

"Thank *you*," she said, awed by the support of this town that was now her home, deep in her heart. "Thanks so much to all of you," she said, glancing at Carrie, Peter, Chad, and the others. "I'm so grateful to you for accepting me in Ardor Creek."

"You're one of us now, honey!" Carrie called. "We've got our claws in you."

Throwing her head back, Ashlyn laughed, finally embracing her future and the knowledge she was going to thrive. There was no other option when you were surrounded by such love and genuine friendship. Sliding her arm around Scott's waist, she held tight, thrilled for the new journeys ahead.

Chapter 25

♥

Ashlyn was pleasantly exhausted by the time the last tour group left on Sunday evening. After showing them the attic, where the children—and maybe some of the adults—had been enthralled by Sally's story, she'd led them down to the truck and served food to those who were hungry. She'd decided to offer it for free to build some goodwill but most of the locals had thrown ample donations into the jar that sat upon her counter. Once everyone departed, she closed up the food truck and headed to the attic, feeling a bit nostalgic for some reason.

"Hey," Scott said, climbing up the attic stairs and walking toward her. "Why are you standing in the dark?"

"The candle's still lit," she said, nodding toward the lone candle burning beside Sally's chair. "I love the atmosphere."

"You made it through your first fall festival and your first year on the haunted homes tour," he said, sliding his arms around her waist. "Did you enjoy it?"

"I loved it," she said, resting her head on his chest as they gazed at Sally's chair. "I swear, it rocked a few times this weekend as I was giving the tours."

"Creepy."

"Yeah." Staring up at him, she squinted. "Mr. Grillo, I can't believe I'm saying this but I think you finally believe in ghosts. Sally would be proud."

"I believe in *you*," he said, placing a sweet kiss on her lips. "And that those we've loved in the past want us to be happy."

"I feel like Grandma Jean, Tina, Ella, and Sally are having a party somewhere that's *really* fun. We're lucky to have had them in our lives."

He nodded as she tucked her head back into the crook of his arm, loving how solid he was against her. Suddenly, as they gazed upon the chair, it creaked and Ashlyn swore it rocked back a centimeter before falling back into place. Scott stiffened as the candle flickered.

"Did you see that?" she whispered.

"Mm-hmm..."

"Holy shit."

Stroking her hair, he kissed her temple. "Okay, your stoic contractor can only take so many ghosts for one day. Let's go to bed."

Chuckling, she grabbed his hand and followed him downstairs. Once the doors were locked and the house was dark, they undressed each other in the soft light of the bedside lamp. Naked and aroused, Ashlyn slid on the bed, fanning her hair over the pillow. Crooking her finger, she beckoned to her lover.

Scott anchored a knee on either side of her hips, resting his palms flat as he loomed over her. "I was so afraid I'd lost the chance to kiss you again," he whispered, brushing a feather-light kiss on her lips.

Nuzzling his nose, she shook her head. "You can kiss me anywhere." Threading her fingers through his hair, she gently directed him lower. "*Everywhere...*"

So in tune with her desires, her lover trailed his lips over her collarbone, the wet path leading to her straining nipple. Closing his lips around the bud, he sucked it into his warm mouth as her eyes closed in pleasure.

Slick, sticky sounds pervaded the room as he lavished her breast while deep, low-toned groans exited his throat. The tiny grunts sparked pinpoints of desire in every cell of her inflamed skin. Moving to her other breast, he devoured it as the hard ridge of his cock jutted against her thigh, driving her mad with lust.

Moving lower, he kneeled before her, sliding his palms over her inner thighs before pushing them apart. Eyes locked with hers, he extended his tongue, stroking her flushed slit slowly and thoroughly before landing on her clit. Flicking it in a maddening rhythm, she melted beneath him, clenching her fingers in his hair as he moaned.

"Yeah, honey," he murmured, kissing her mound. "Pull me into that sweet pussy."

"Oh, god," she cried, tugging him closer to her core. "Scott..."

"You taste so good, sweetheart." Sliding his tongue through her drenched folds, he alternated between teasing the tight ring of her slick opening and flicking her clit. Mired in bliss, Ashlyn caved to the pleasure. Lost in his growls of pleasure and desire, her back arched when he sucked her swollen bud between his lips. Feeling her body snap, she exploded, closing her thighs around his head as he buried his face in her most intimate place.

Struggling to catch her breath, she finally released her death grip on his head, relaxing her legs. Crawling over her, he smiled, brushing the hair off her forehead. "I think you almost smothered me but what a way to go."

Biting her lip, she slung her leg over his ass. "Why don't you punish me, then? I think you need to fuck me really hard."

Eliciting a growl, the head of his cock found her center. Sliding it through her essence, he lubricated himself before gliding inside. "Next time," he whispered. "I have a lot of fantasies I want to indulge with you. But, for now, I just need to feel you."

"I'm here," she said softly, opening herself to him.

"I love you," he said, staring into those magnificent eyes as his cock raked through her tight, wet folds. "I'm going to give you everything, Ash."

"I know you are." Cupping his cheek, she felt the tears form. One slid down her cheek and he kissed it away as his hips undulated into her quaking body. Plunging his tongue into her mouth, he kissed her, thorough and desperate, as she clung to him, feeling his body tense as the pace increased.

Eventually, he groaned as his muscles tightened.

"Fuck, I'm so close, honey...*oh, god...*"

"I love you," she cried, hugging his sweat-soaked skin.

Screaming her name, his head jerked back as his handsome features constricted with pleasure. Collapsing against her, he buried his face in her neck as his body spasmed, jetting warm pulses of desire into hers. Wrapping her legs around him, she clutched his frame, his quakes and shudders sending sparks of sated energy through her depleted body.

"God, you feel so good around me."

She squeezed her inner muscles around his now-sated cock and he groaned. "You're doing that on purpose."

Chuckling, she nodded. "Busted."

Lifting his head, he smiled. "I'm so glad we ditched the condoms."

"Me too." She waggled her eyebrows.

Tracing her face with his finger, he rested his head on his hand, his elbow anchored into the mattress. "Pretty soon, I'm going to ask you to marry me. After that, maybe we can ditch the IUD too?"

"Why, Mr. Grillo, are you proposing marriage and babies to me? I just wanted you for your contracting skills."

Breathing a laugh, he gave her a sloppy kiss. "I'll build you a hundred damn houses as long as you say 'yes'. But I want to plan something special and buy you the perfect ring. I'd also like to surprise you."

"How romantic," she sighed, raking her fingers through his hair, the scratch of her nails on his scalp eliciting tremors from his body.

"You deserve it and, honestly, maybe I do too."

"You do, sweetheart," she said, running her thumb over his lips. "We've both had so much pain. Let's decide to be happy."

"Okay, but on one condition."

"Yeah?"

"You make me meatloaf and chocolate cake once per month, minimum."

Throwing her head back on the pillow, she laughed. "Deal. You drive a tough bargain, Mr. Grillo."

"Just you wait, city girl. You ain't seen nothing yet." Lowering his lips to hers, he inhaled her giggles as they lost themselves in their newfound phase of love.

Epilogue

♥

Three years later…

Ashlyn held the little boy on her hip and pointed at the picture. "Who's that?" she asked.

"Ella!"

"That's right. And who's that?" She pointed to the woman holding his sister in the photo.

"Ella's mommy."

"Ella's mommy," she said, rubbing his nose with hers. "Tina. Can you say 'Tina?'"

"Tina," Grant said.

"You're so smart. Remember you get that from your mommy," she whispered, playfully tickling his tummy.

"I heard that," Scott said, entering the living room and giving a playful eye roll. Leaning down, he kissed her forehead and then his son's. "But I'll let it slide since you're about to burst."

Rubbing her hand over her distended abdomen, Ashlyn sighed. "I look like a freaking whale. Whose idea was it to get pregnant again so fast?"

Squinting, he looked at the ceiling. "Not sure. It probably had to do with the fact Mommy couldn't keep her hands off Daddy, right, Grant?" Taking the infant, he lifted him high in the air.

"You wish, buddy." Punching him in the arm, she chuckled when he scrunched his features at her. "But I'll let you live since you remodeled both bedrooms, added on another one, and built this pretty new mantel for me. Ah, the perks of marrying a contractor."

As he held their son, he gazed at her, reverent and tender, causing her to grin up at him.

"What? Do I have something on my face?"

"You just look so beautiful. I'm going to miss you being pregnant."

"That makes one of us," she muttered. Swiping her hands over her green dress, she asked, "Do you like the dress? I could barely get it zipped."

"You look so pretty, honey. Can't wait for the wedding."

"Pretty, Mommy," Grant said.

"Thank you, sweetie," she said, placing a wet kiss on his lips. "Can you believe they're finally tying the knot?"

"Nope. Never thought Chad would take the leap. But there's something in the water in Ardor Creek spurring people to get married. We were just the first to start the trend."

"With Carrie and Peter close behind," she said, lifting a finger.

"Who do you think will take the plunge after Chad?"

"I have my guesses."

Sliding her arm around his waist, she asked, "Want to wager on it?"

"Oh, you're on. What are the terms?"

"Whoever wins gets to knock another fantasy off the list."

His gaze smoldered as she waggled her brows.

"That basically means we both win."

"Mr. Grillo, you're picking up what I'm putting down."

"Well, Mrs. Grillo," he said, "let's get to this wedding and place our bets. Can't wait. Ready, buddy?" he asked, repositioning him on his hip.

"Wedding!" was his excited reply as he clapped his hands.

"That's a yes," Ashlyn said, striding to grab her purse. "I'll drive if you strap him in."

"Done."

Loading into the SUV, the family headed to see the playboy of Ardor Creek marry the love of his life.

Before You Go

♥

Thanks so much for starting this new series with me! I hope you enjoyed Scott and Ashlyn's story and found it as poignant and heartfelt as I did. Carrie and Peter are next and, wow, their book has a HUGE surprise. You can read their book, **Illusions Unveiled**, right now! Thanks for spending some time in Ardor Creek with me!

Please consider leaving a review on your retailer's site, BookBub, and/or Goodreads. Your reviews help spread the word for indie authors so we can keep writing smokin' hot books for you to devour. Thanks so much for reading!

About the Author

♥

Ayla Asher is the pen name for a USA Today bestselling author who writes steamy fantasy romance under a different pseudonym. However, she loves a spicy, fast-paced contemporary romance too! Therefore, she's decided to share some of her contemporary stories, hoping to spread a little joy one HEA at a time. She would love to connect with you on social media, where she enjoys making dorky TikToks, FB/IG posts and fun book trailers!

Also by Ayla Asher

Manhattan Holiday Loves Trilogy

Book 1: His Holiday Pact

Book 2: Her Valentine Surprise

Book 3: Her Patriotic Prince

Ardor Creek Series

Book 1: Hearts Reclaimed

Book 2: Illusions Unveiled

Book 3: Desires Uncovered

Book 4: Resolutions Embraced

Book 5: Passions Fulfilled

Book 6: Futures Entwined